Augel's Young Mozart

BiG

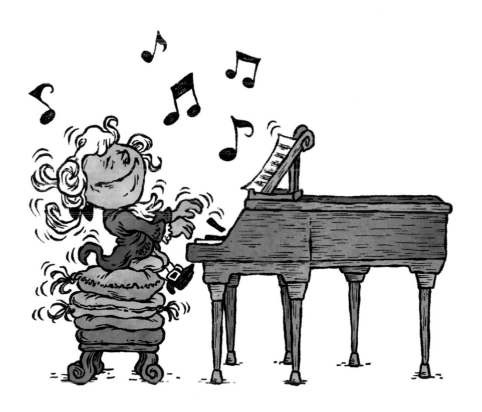

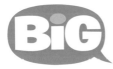

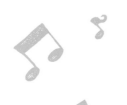

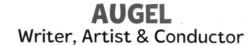

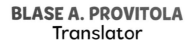

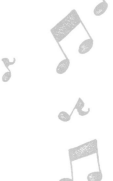

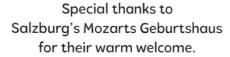

AUGEL
Writer, Artist & Conductor

•

BLASE A. PROVITOLA
Translator

•

FABRICE SAPOLSKY
ALEX DONOGHUE
US Edition Editors

AMANDA LUCIDO
Assistant Editor

VINCENT HENRY
Original Edition Editor

JERRY FRISSEN
Senior Art Director

FABRICE GIGER
Publisher

Rights and Licensing - licensing@humanoids.com
Press and Social Media - pr@humanoids.com

Special thanks to
Salzburg's Mozarts Geburtshaus
for their warm welcome.

YOUNG MOZART. This title is a publication of Humanoids, Inc. 8033 Sunset Blvd. #628, Los Angeles, CA 90046.

Library of Congress Control Number: 2018956925

BIG is an imprint of Humanoids, Inc.

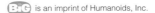

Who's Who?

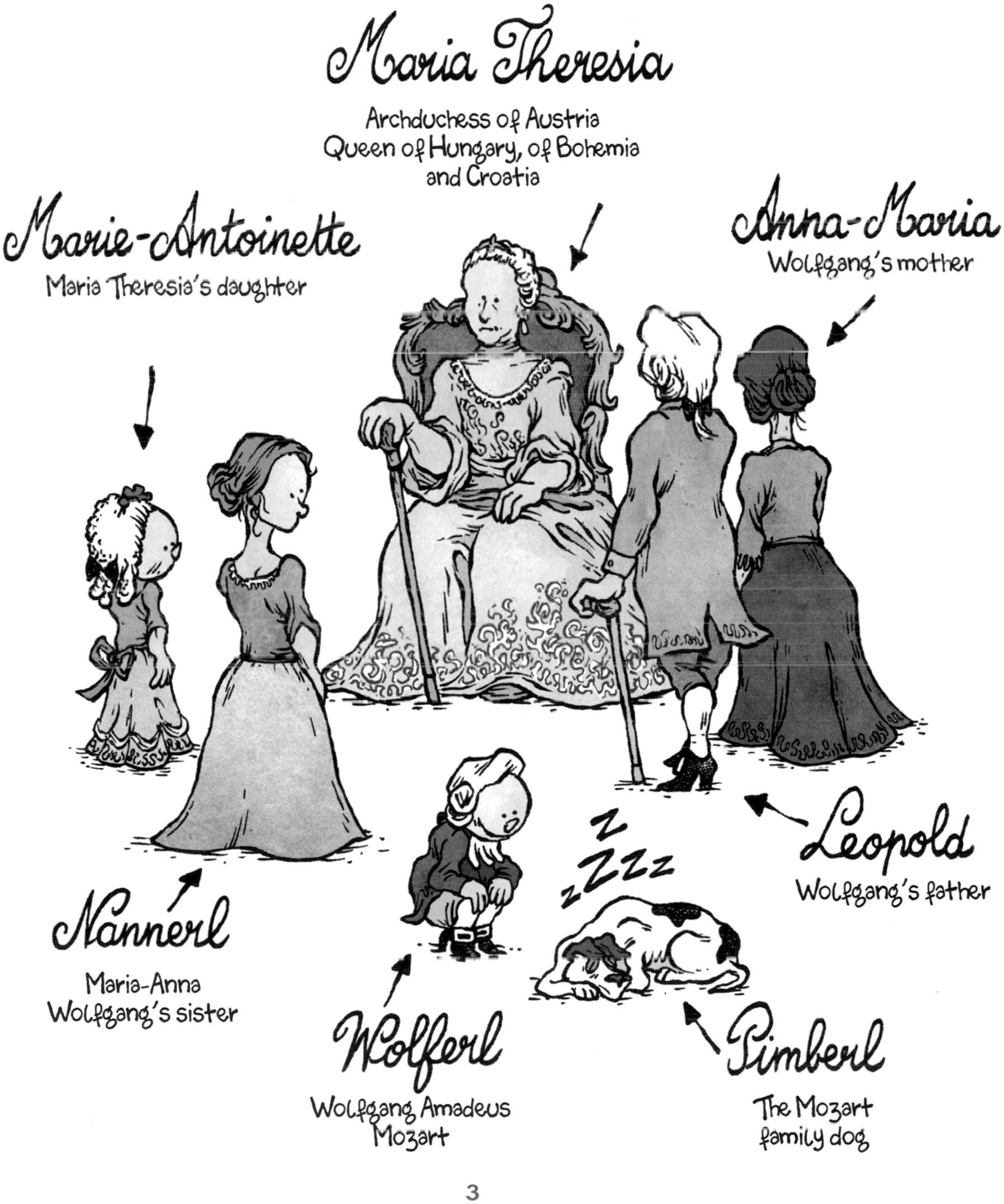
Maria Theresia
Archduchess of Austria
Queen of Hungary, of Bohemia
and Croatia
Marie-Antoinette
Maria Theresia's daughter
Anna-Maria
Wolfgang's mother
Leopold
Wolfgang's father
Nannerl
Maria-Anna
Wolfgang's sister
Wolferl
Wolfgang Amadeus
Mozart
Pimberl
The Mozart
family dog
zZZzz

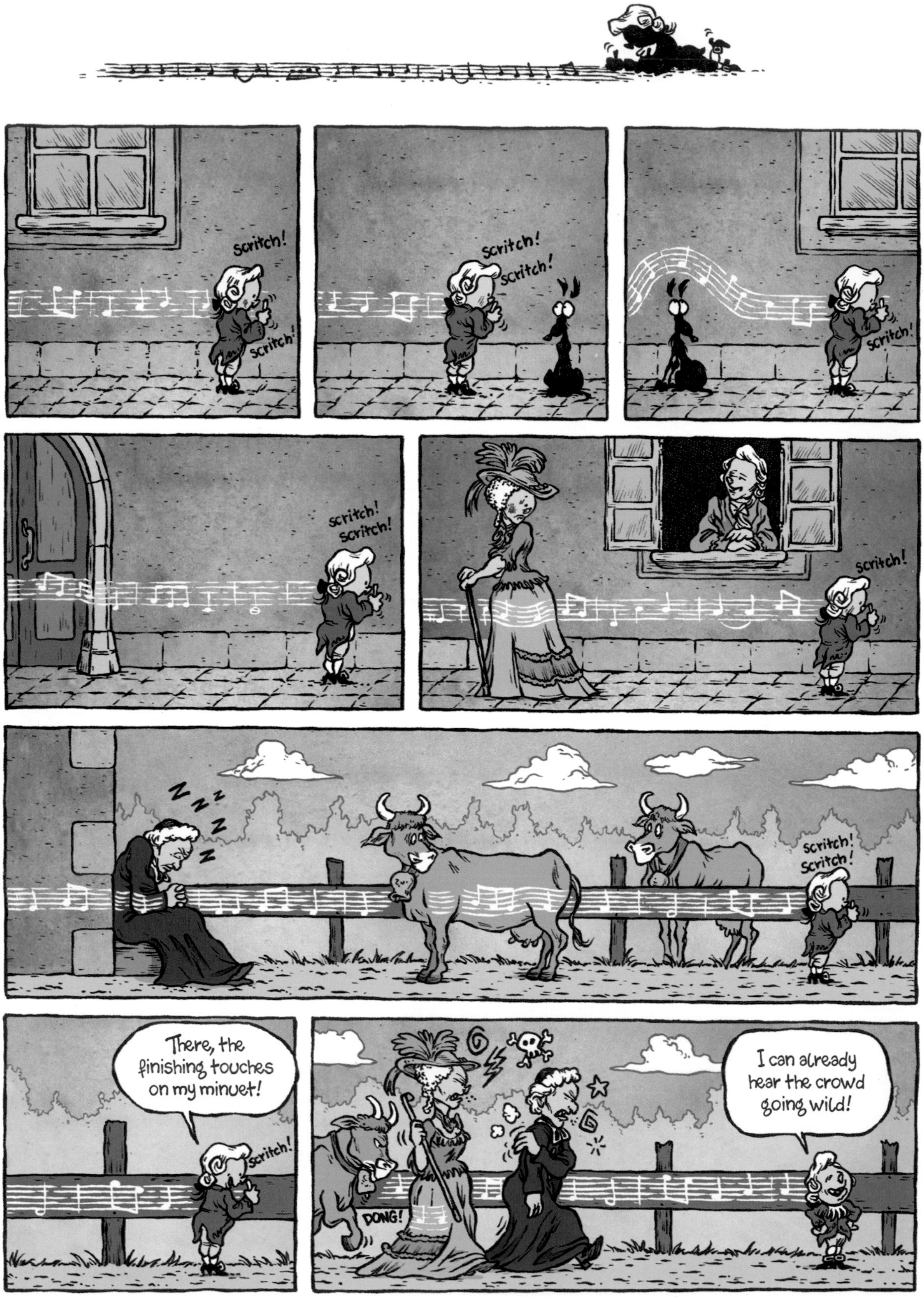
Scritch!
Scritch!
Scritch!
Scritch!
Scritch!
Scritch!
Scritch!
Scritch!
Scritch!
Scritch!
Scritch!
ZZZZ
There, the finishing touches on my minuet!
Scritch!
DONG!
I can already hear the crowd going wild!

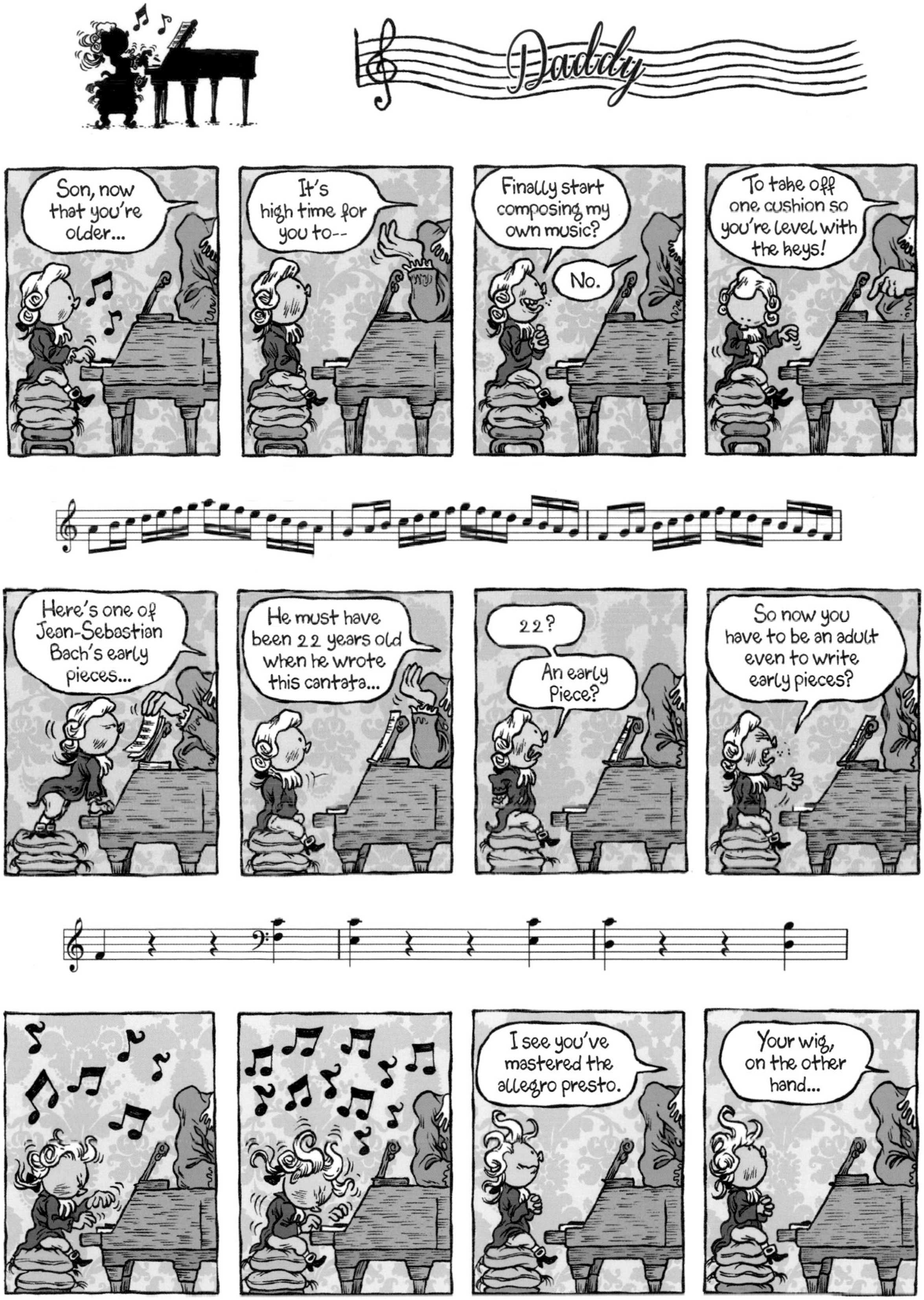
Daddy
Son, now that you're older...
It's high time for you to--
Finally start composing my own music?
No.
To take off one cushion so you're level with the keys!
Here's one of Jean-Sebastian Bach's early pieces...
He must have been 22 years old when he wrote this cantata...
22?
An early Piece?
So now you have to be an adult even to write early pieces?
I see you've mastered the allegro presto.
Your wig, on the other hand...

6

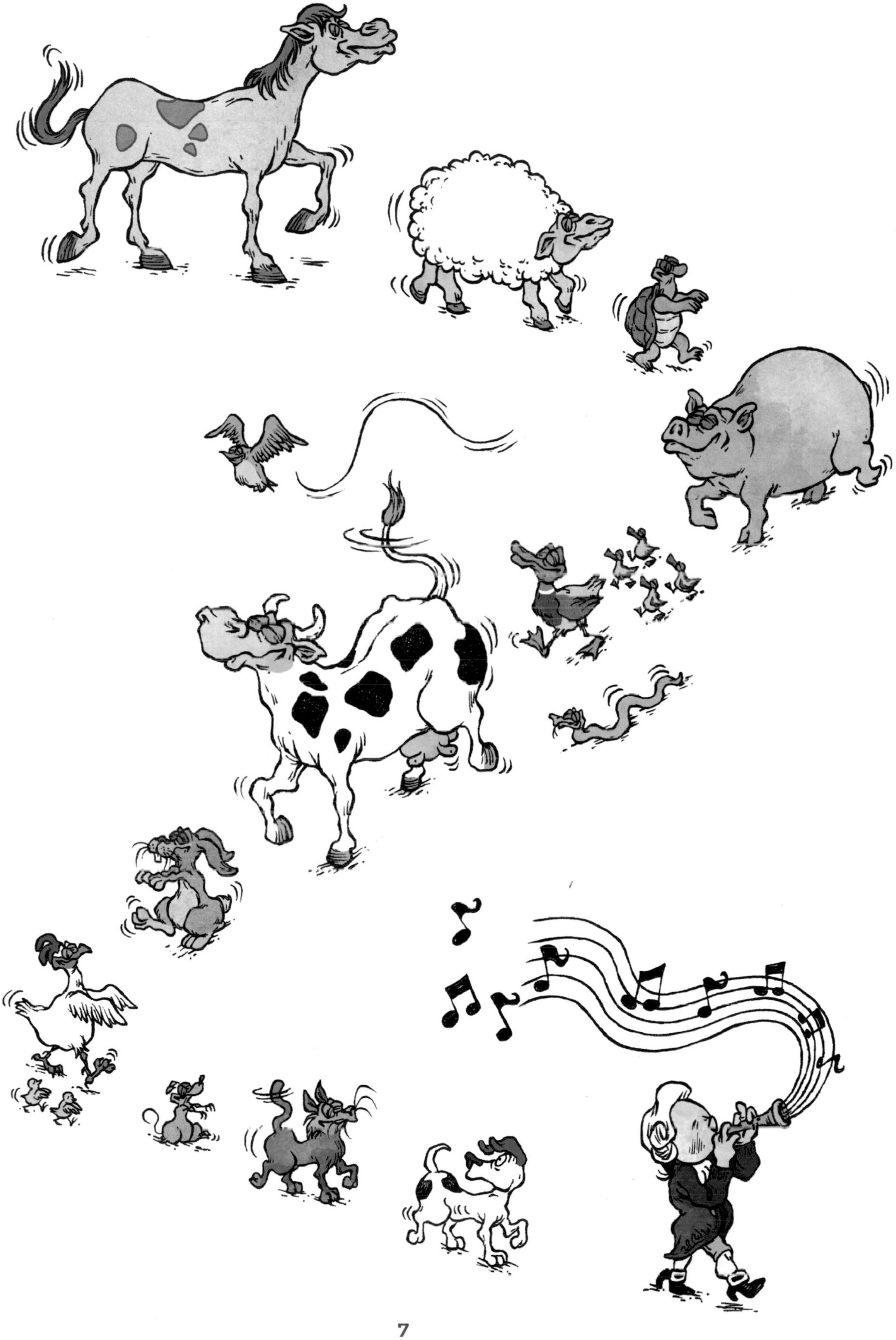

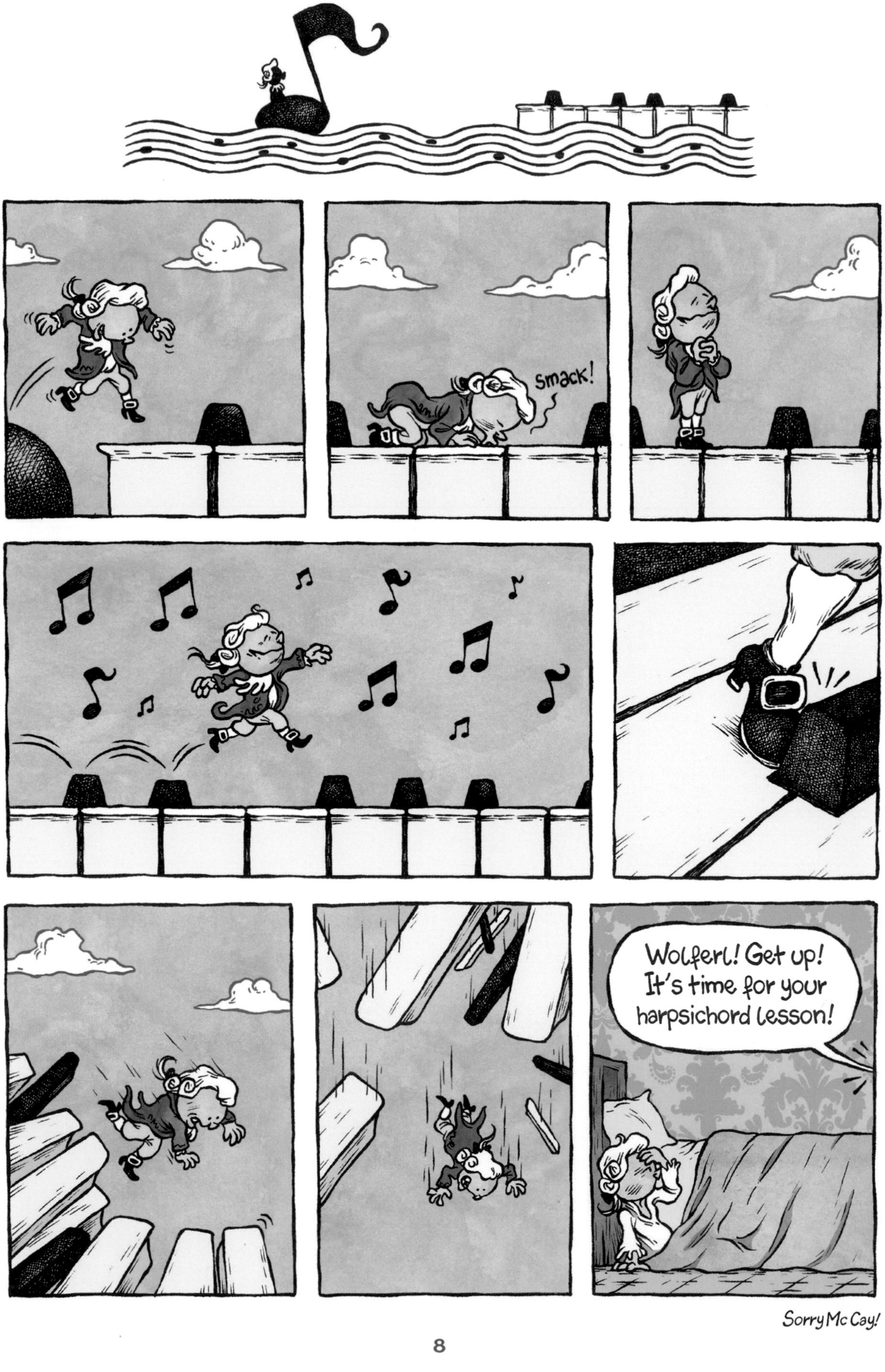
SMACK!
Wolferl! Get up! It's time for your harpsichord lesson!
Sorry McCay!

Acoustics

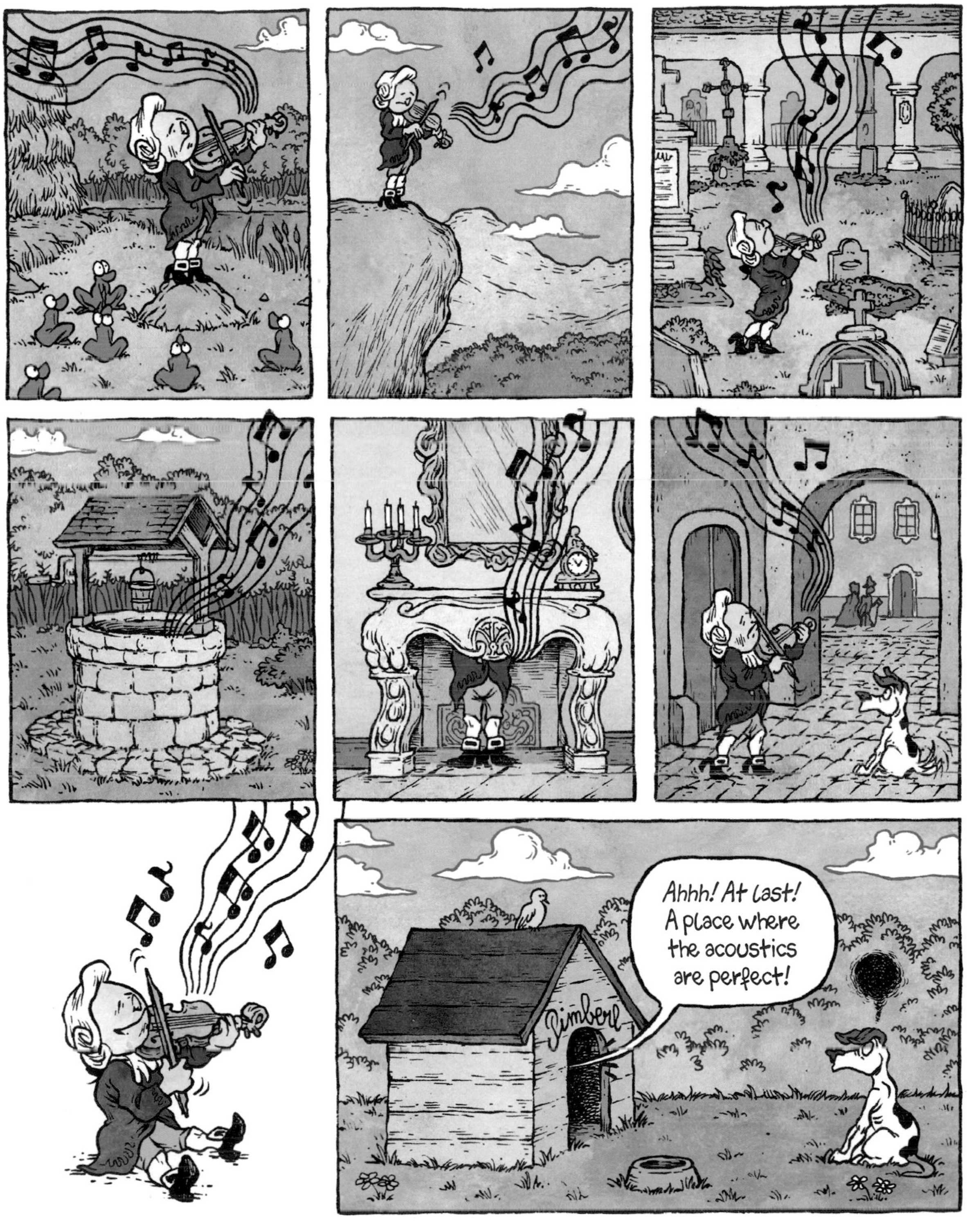
Ahhh! At last! A place where the acoustics are perfect!

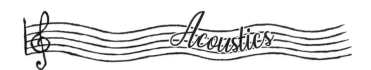

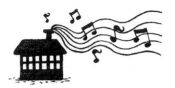

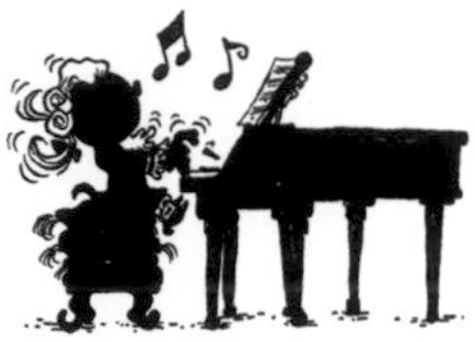

Daddy Too

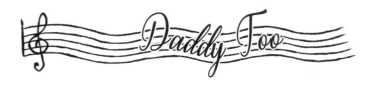

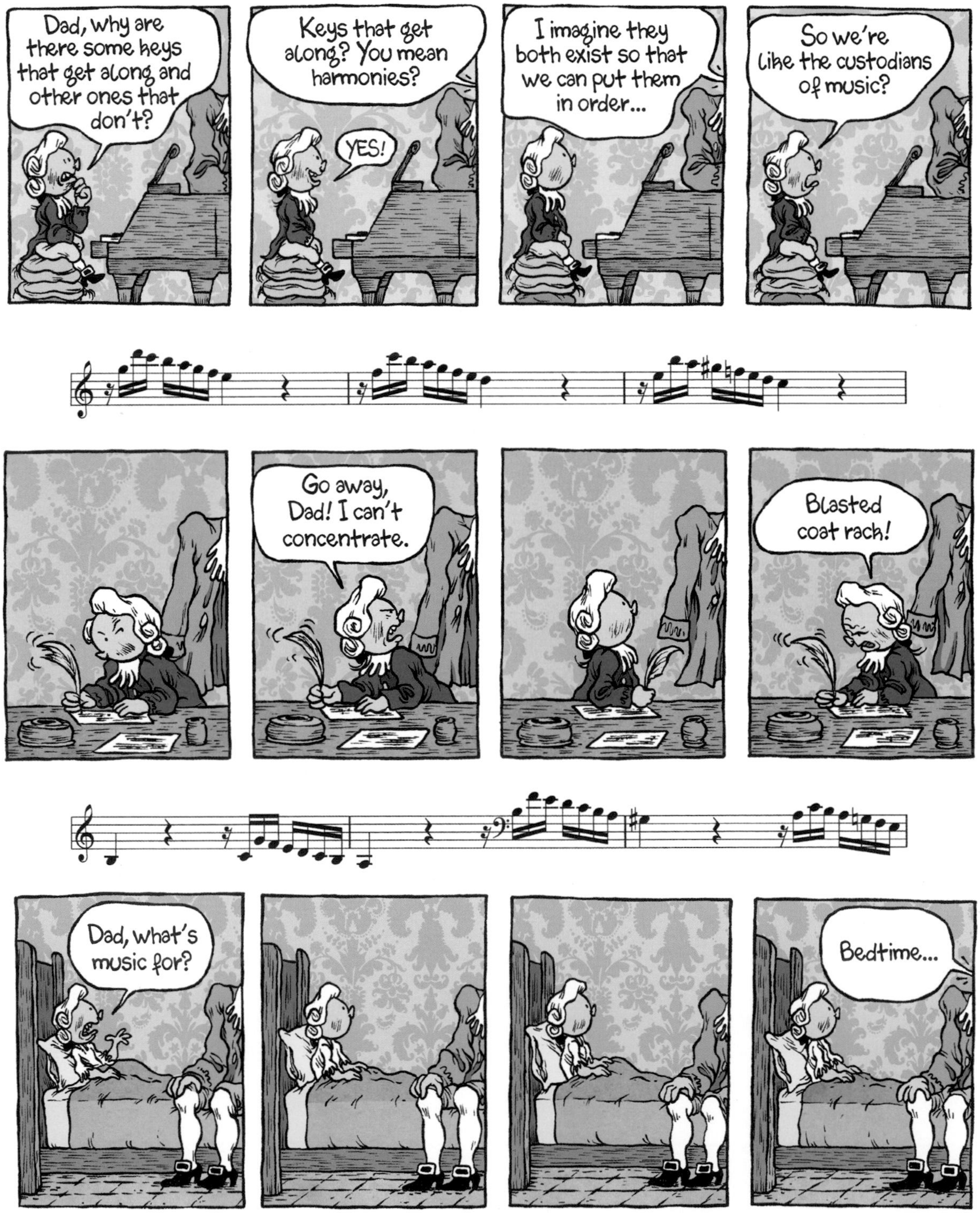
Dad, why are there some keys that get along and other ones that don't?
Keys that get along? You mean harmonies?
YES!
I imagine they both exist so that we can put them in order...
So we're like the custodians of music?
Go away, Dad! I can't concentrate.
Blasted coat rack!
Dad, what's music for?
Bedtime...

Tap Dancing

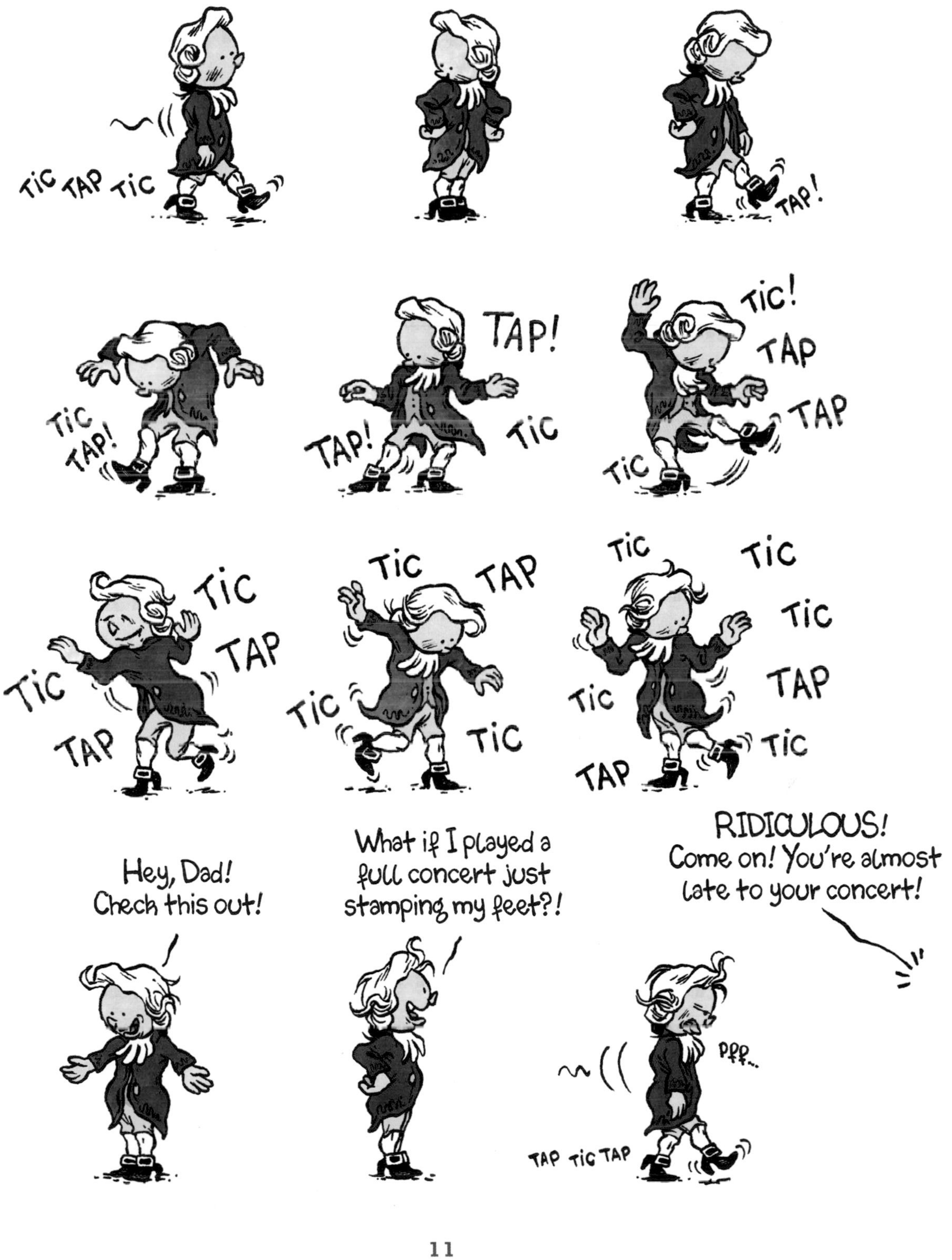
TIC TAP TIC
TAP!
TIC TAP!
TAP!
TAP! TIC
TIC! TAP TAP TIC
TIC TAP TIC TAP
TIC TAP TIC TIC
TIC TIC TIC TIC TAP TAP TIC
Hey, Dad! Check this out!
What if I played a full concert just stamping my feet?!
RIDICULOUS! Come on! You're almost late to your concert!
Pff...
TAP TIC TAP

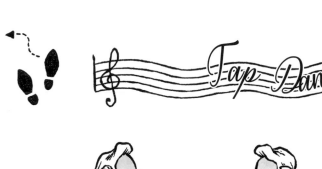

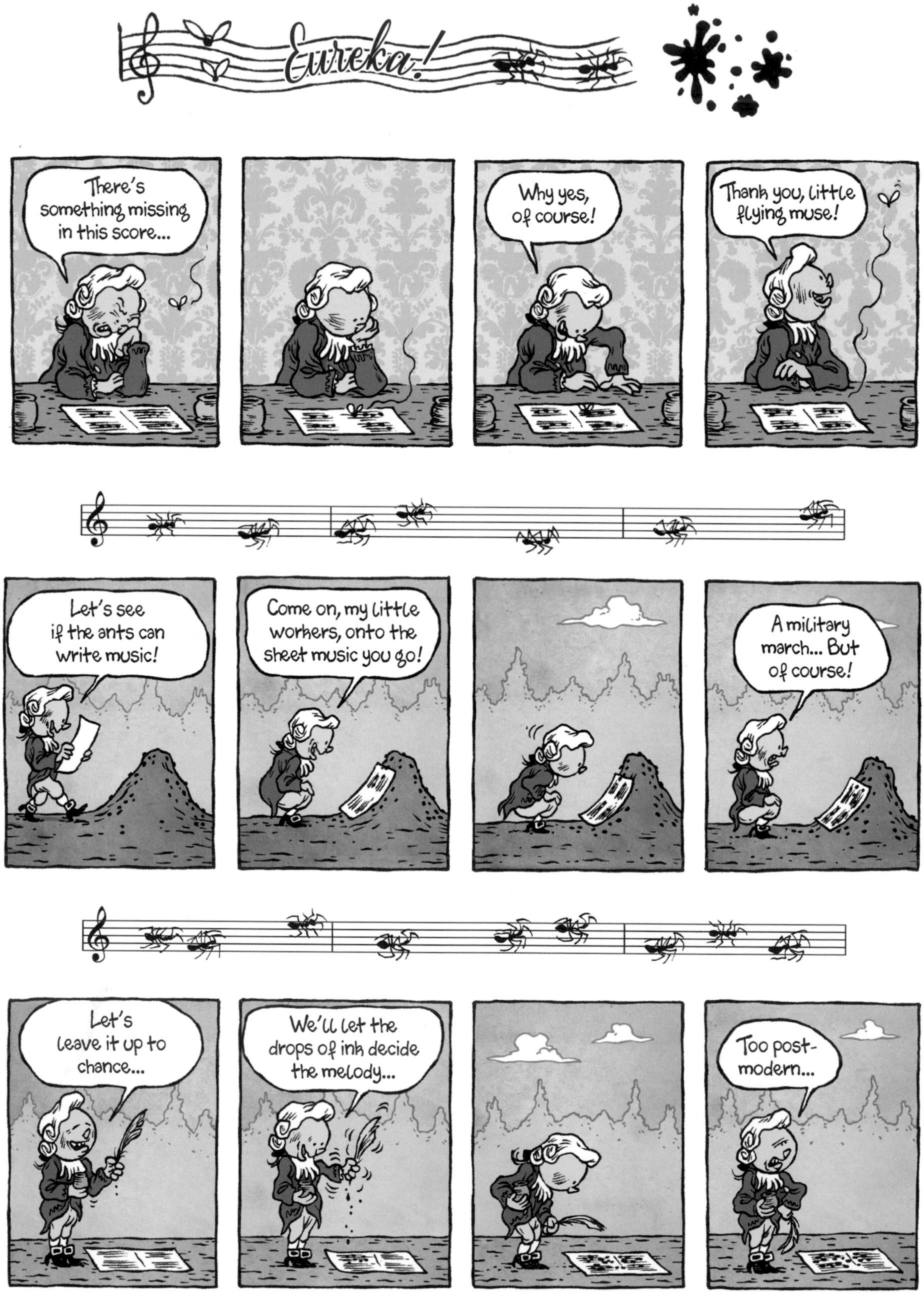
Eureka!
There's something missing in this score...
Why yes, of course!
Thank you, little flying muse!
Let's see if the ants can write music!
Come on, my little workers, onto the sheet music you go!
A military march... But of course!
Let's leave it up to chance...
We'll let the drops of ink decide the melody...
Too post-modern...

A Day in the Life

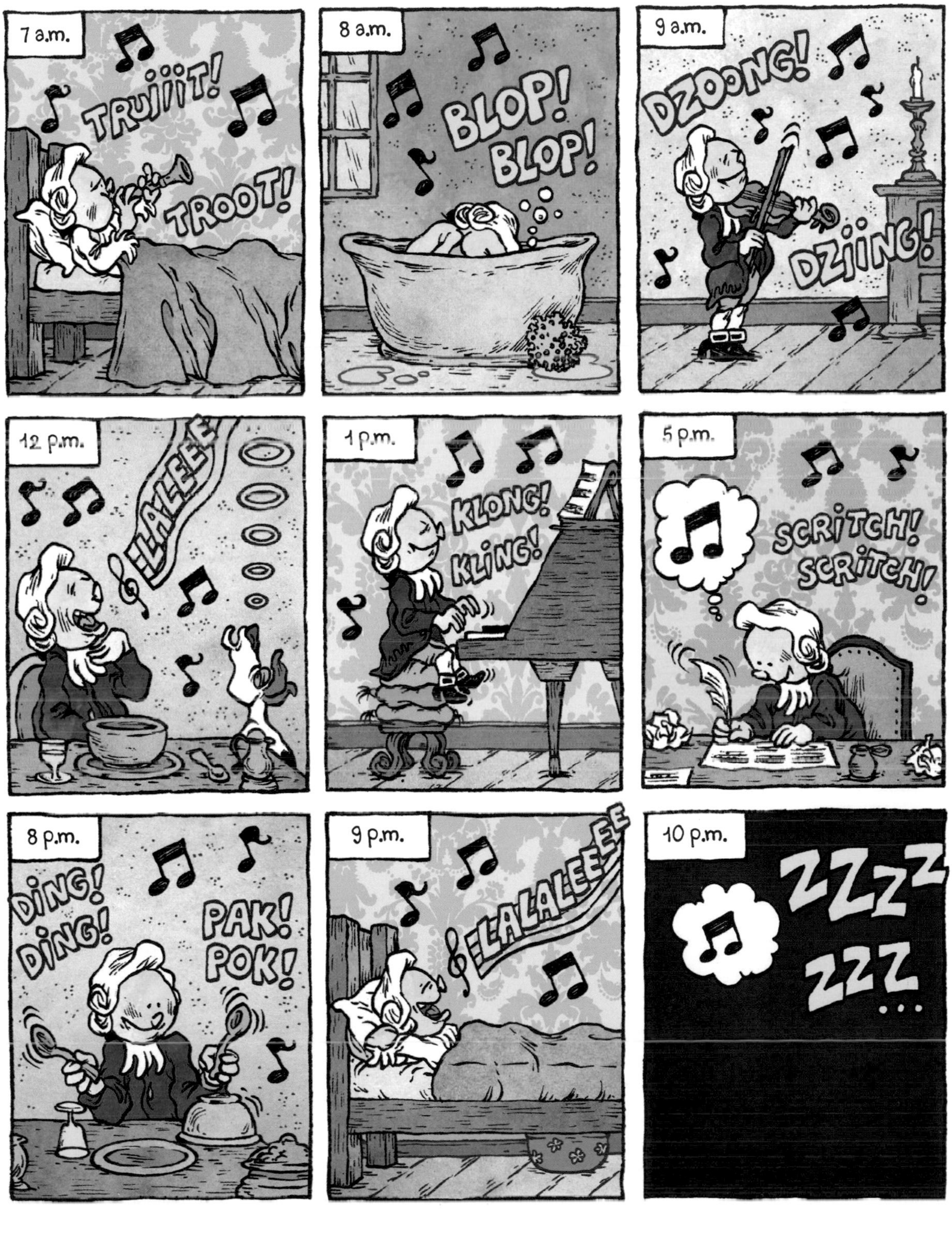
7 a.m.
TRUIIIT!
TROOT!
8 a.m.
BLOP! BLOP!
9 a.m.
DZOOONG!
DZIING!
12 p.m.
LALEEE
1 p.m.
KLONG! KLING!
5 p.m.
SCRITCH! SCRITCH!
8 p.m.
DING! DING!
PAK! POK!
9 p.m.
LALALEEEEE
10 p.m.
ZZZZ
ZZZ...

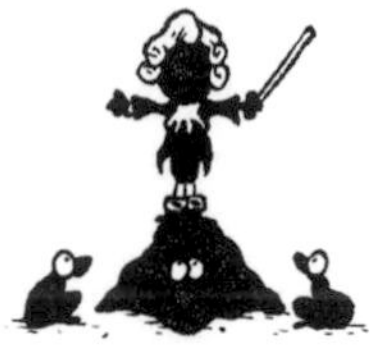

Ribbit Ribbit

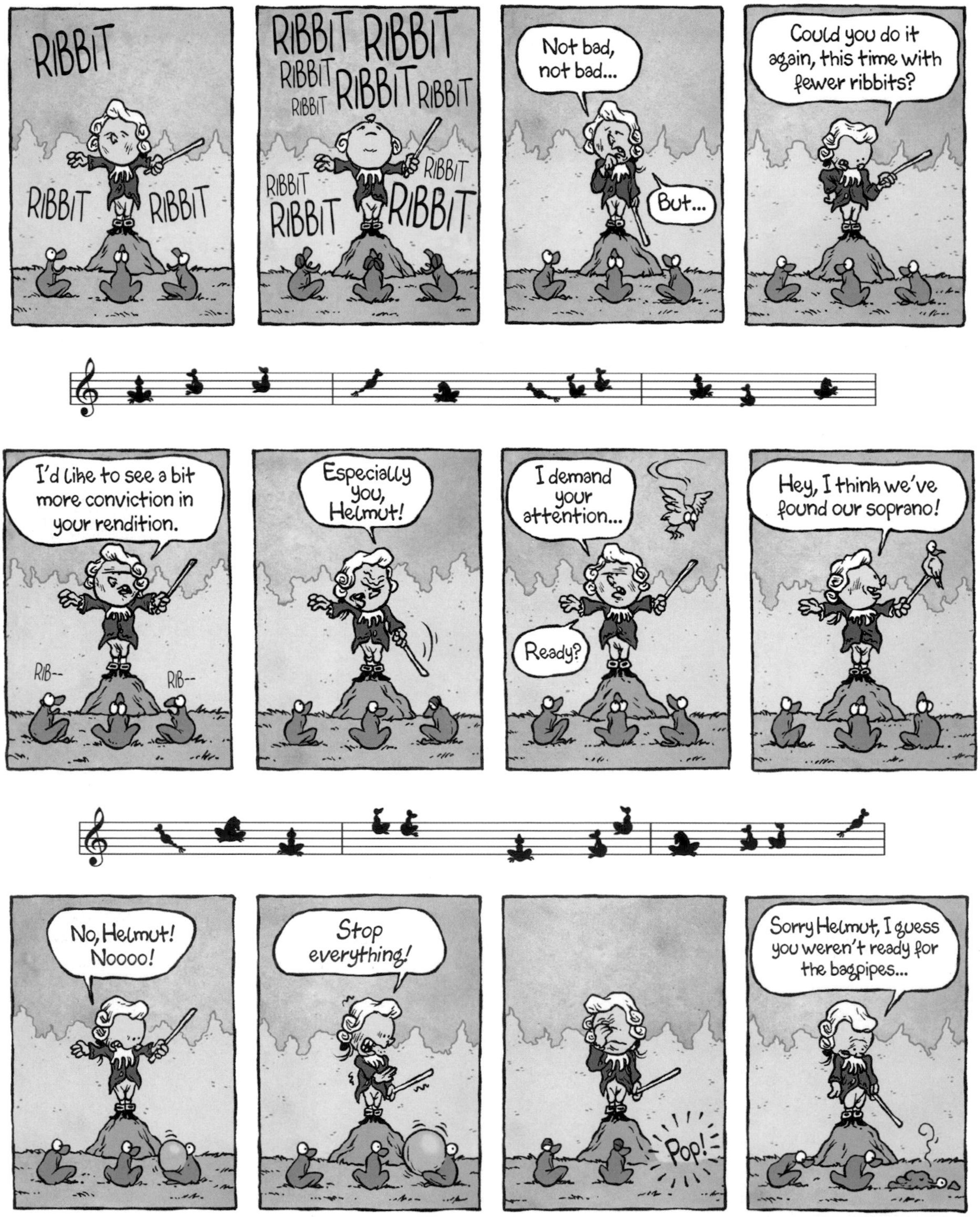
RIBBIT
RIBBIT RIBBIT
RIBBIT RIBBIT RIBBIT RIBBIT RIBBIT RIBBIT RIBBIT RIBBIT RIBBIT
Not bad, not bad...
But...
Could you do it again, this time with fewer ribbits?
I'd like to see a bit more conviction in your rendition.
RIB-- RIB--
Especially you, Helmut!
I demand your attention...
Ready?
Hey, I think we've found our soprano!
No, Helmut! Noooo!
Stop everything!
Pop!
Sorry Helmut, I guess you weren't ready for the bagpipes...

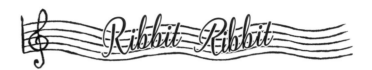

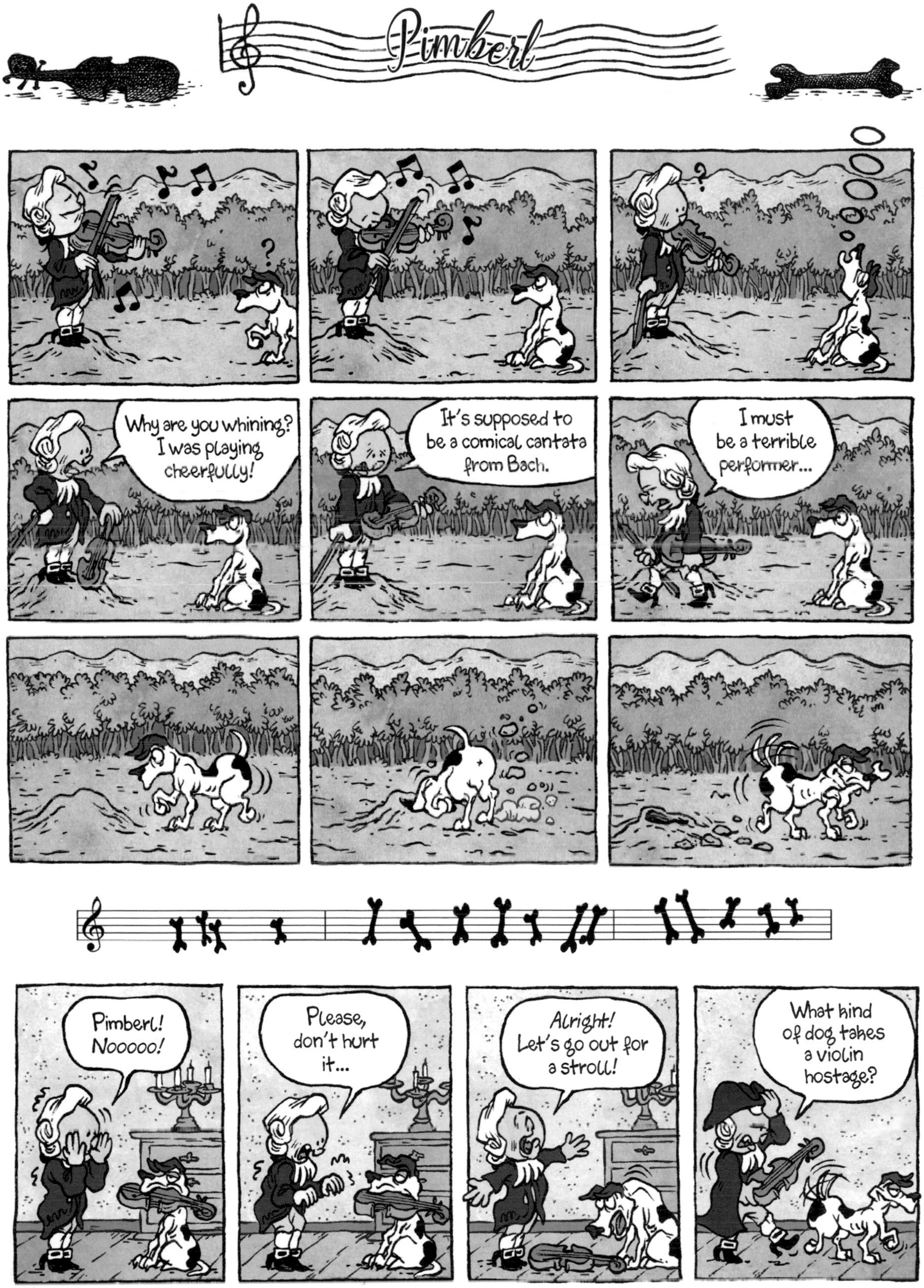
Pimberl
Why are you whining? I was playing cheerfully!
It's supposed to be a comical cantata from Bach.
I must be a terrible performer...
Pimberl! Nooooo!
Please, don't hurt it...
Alright! Let's go out for a stroll!
What kind of dog takes a violin hostage?

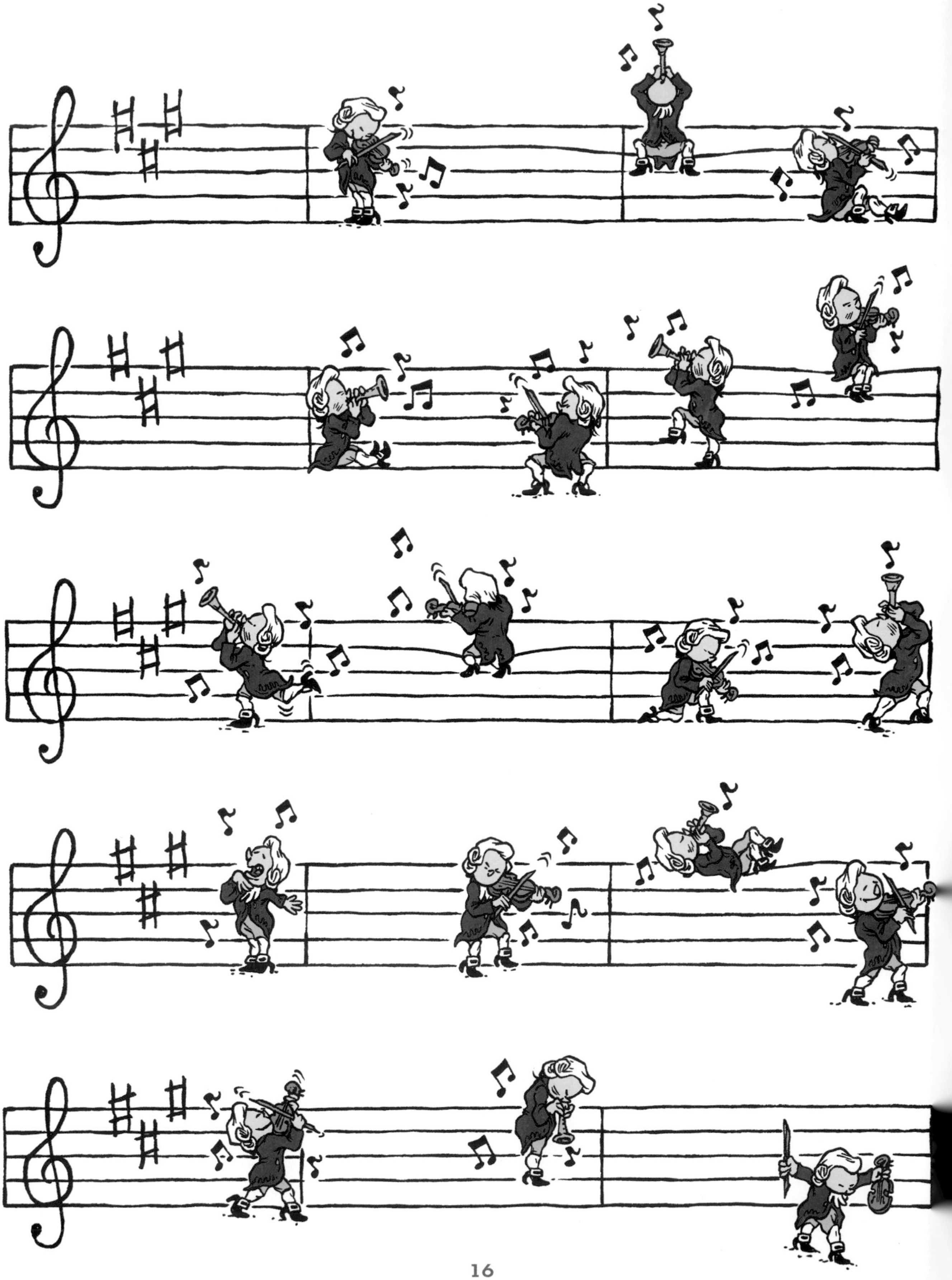

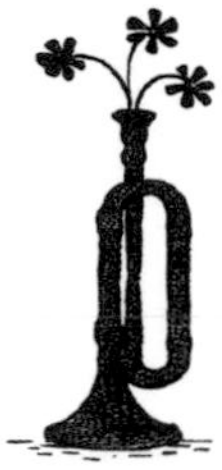

The Trumpet

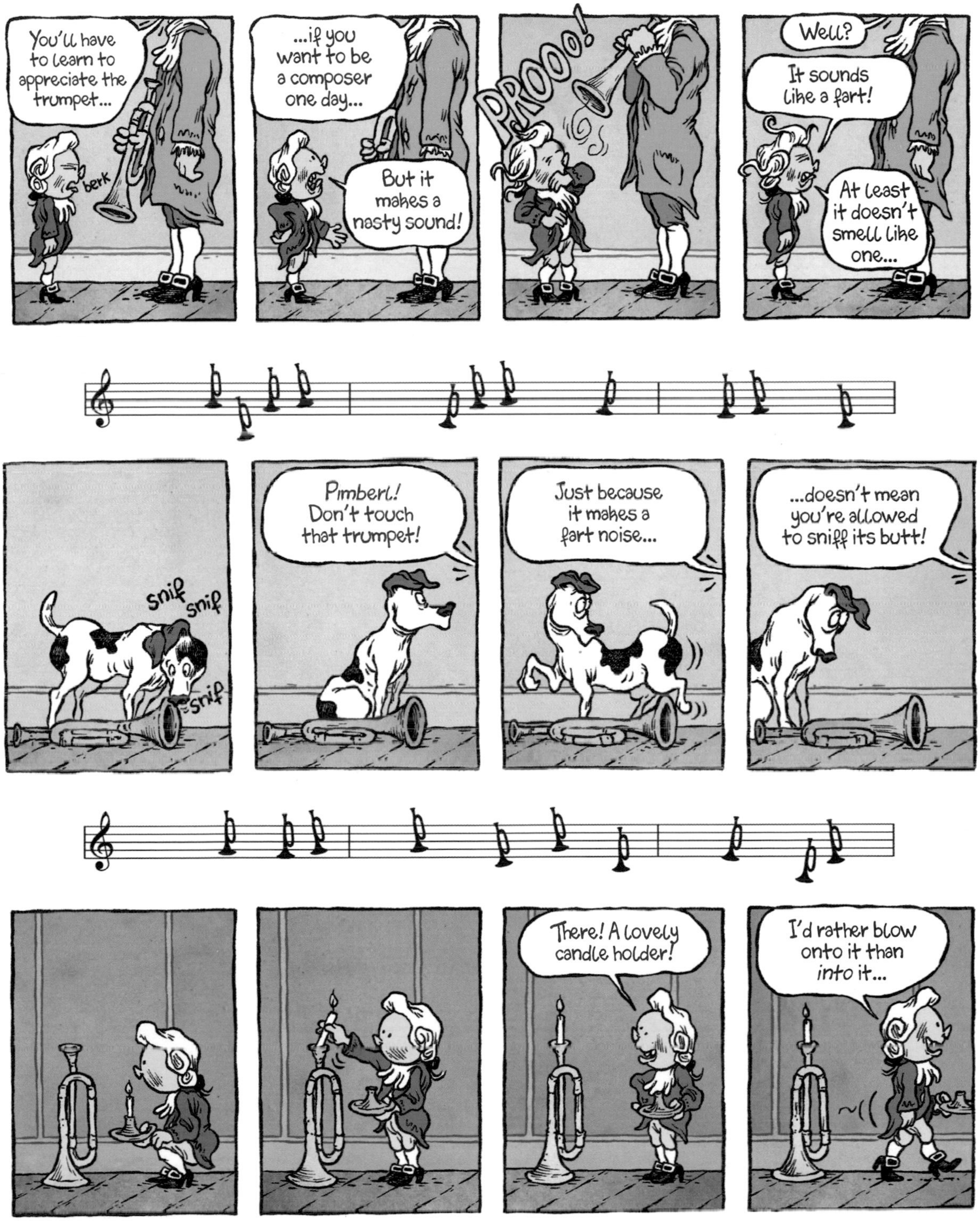

You'll have to learn to appreciate the trumpet...
berk
...if you want to be a composer one day...
But it makes a nasty sound!
PROOOO!
Well?
It sounds like a fart!
At least it doesn't smell like one...
snif snif
snif
Pimberl! Don't touch that trumpet!
Just because it makes a fart noise...
...doesn't mean you're allowed to sniff its butt!
There! A lovely candle holder!
I'd rather blow onto it than *into* it...

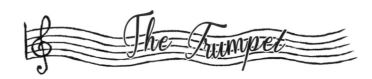

Immature

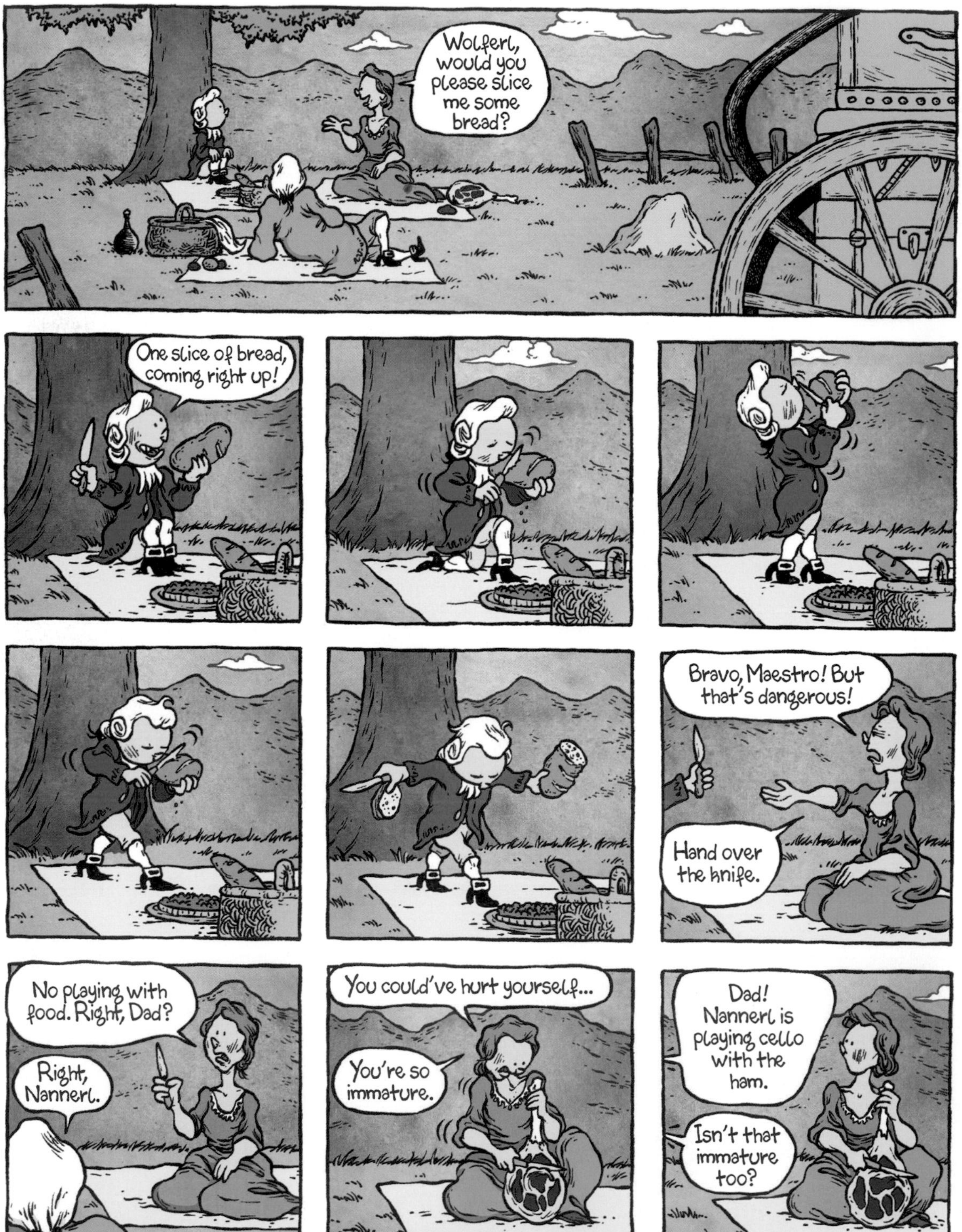

Wolferl, would you please slice me some bread?
One slice of bread, coming right up!
Bravo, Maestro! But that's dangerous!
Hand over the knife.
No playing with food. Right, Dad?
Right, Nannerl.
You could've hurt yourself...
You're so immature.
Dad! Nannerl is playing cello with the ham.
Isn't that immature too?

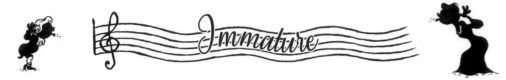

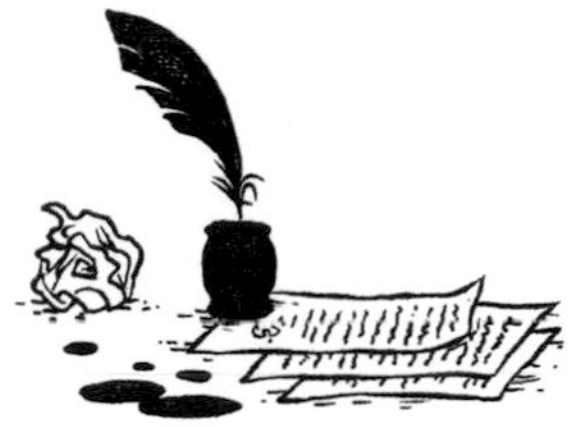

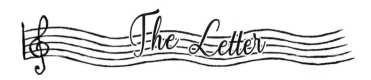

The Letter

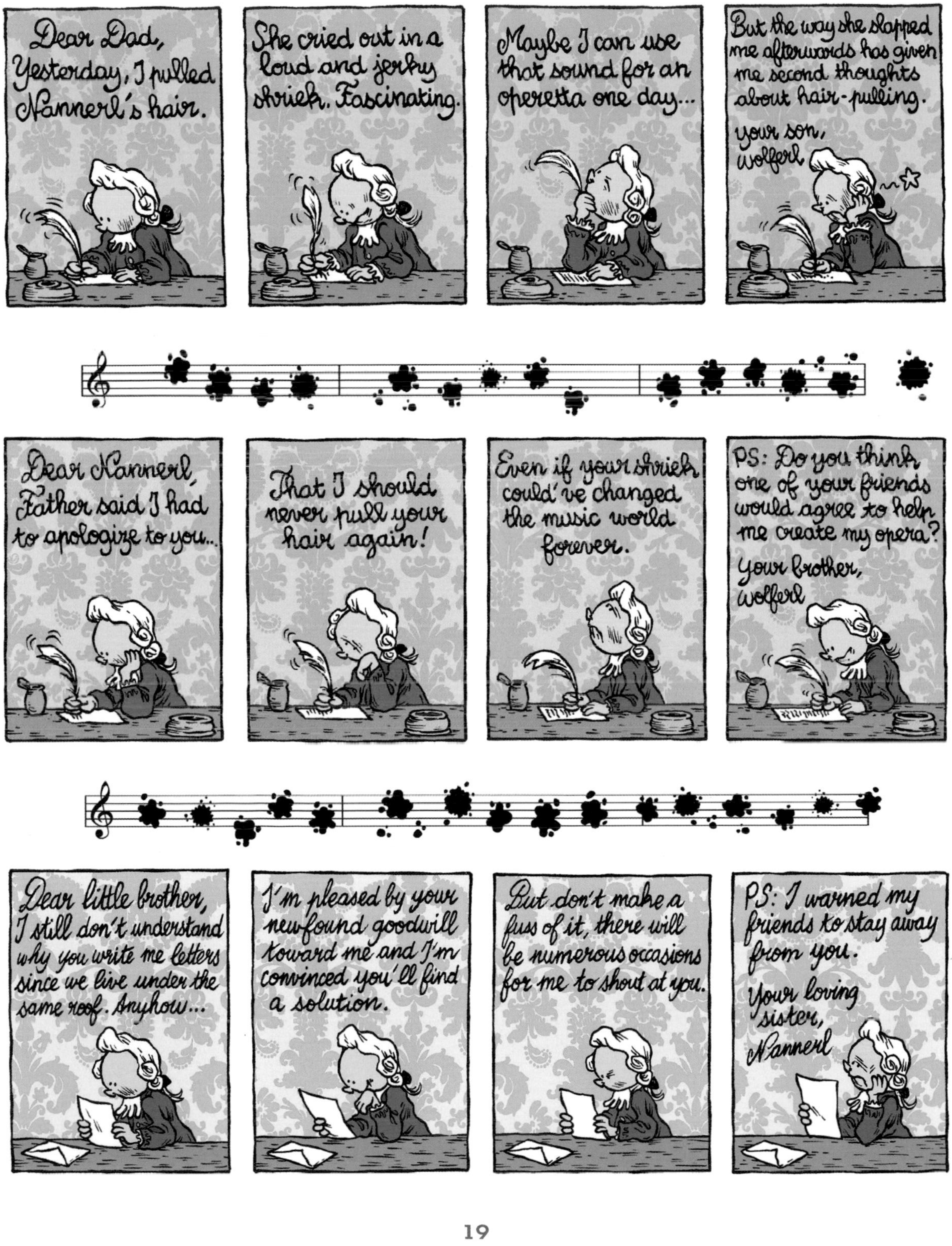
Dear Dad,
Yesterday, I pulled Nannerl's hair.
She cried out in a loud and jerky shriek. Fascinating.
Maybe I can use that sound for an operetta one day...
But the way she slapped me afterwards has given me second thoughts about hair-pulling.
your son,
wolferl
Dear Nannerl,
Father said I had to apologize to you...
That I should never pull your hair again!
Even if your shriek could've changed the music world forever.
PS: Do you think one of your friends would agree to help me create my opera?
Your brother,
wolferl
Dear little brother,
I still don't understand why you write me letters since we live under the same roof. Anyhow...
I'm pleased by your newfound goodwill toward me and I'm convinced you'll find a solution.
But don't make a fuss of it, there will be numerous occasions for me to shout at you.
PS: I warned my friends to stay away from you.
Your loving sister,
Nannerl

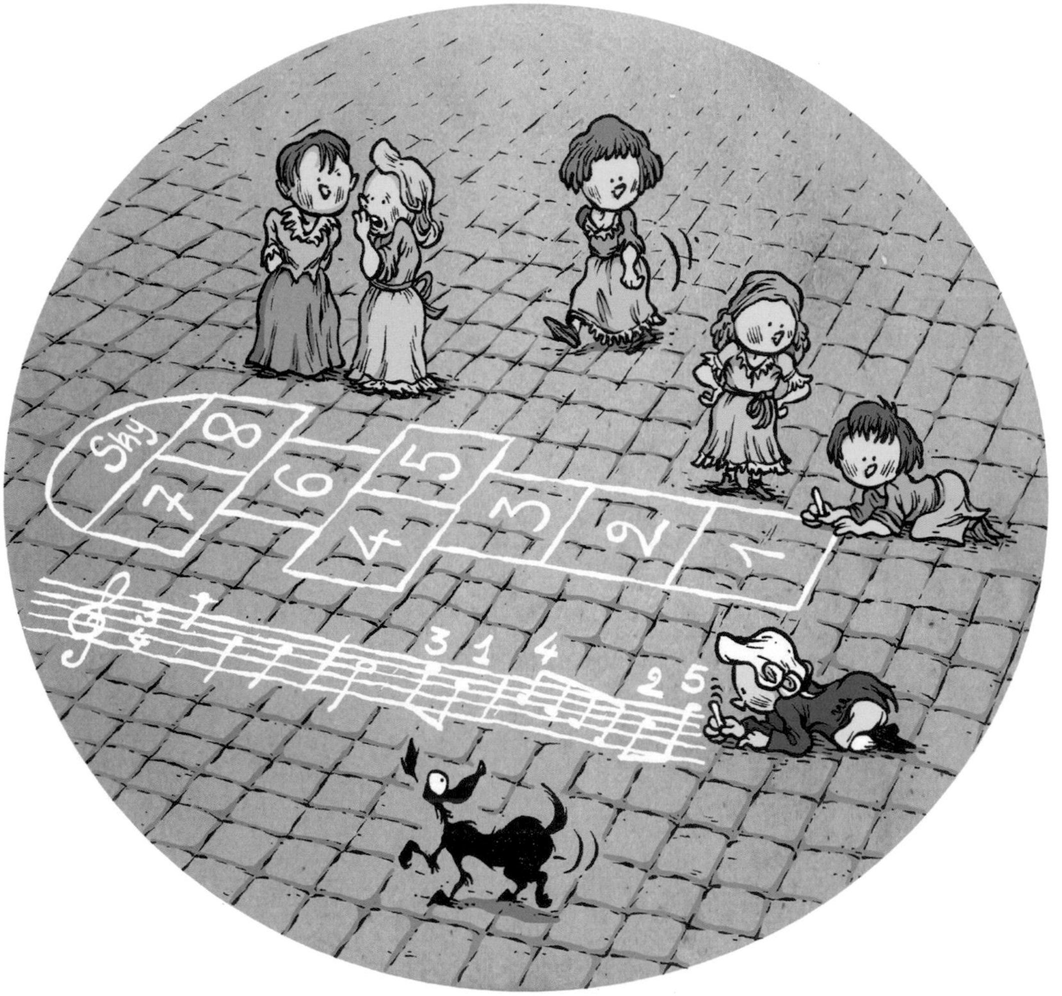
Sky
8
7
6
5
4
3
2
1
3 1 4
2 5

The Beverage

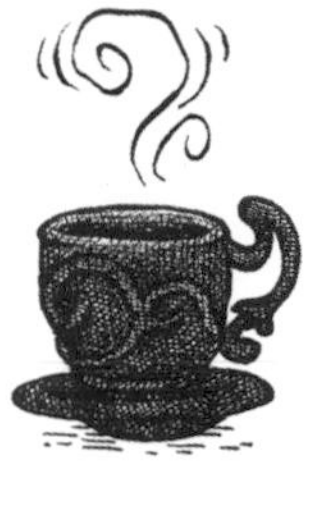

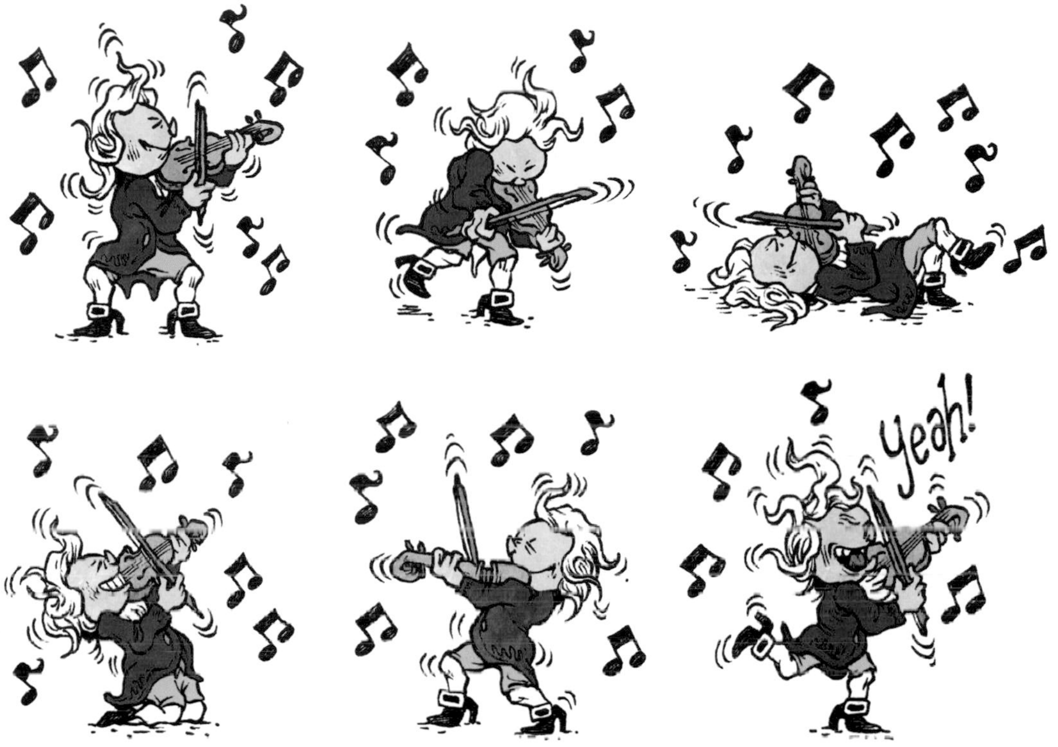

yeah!

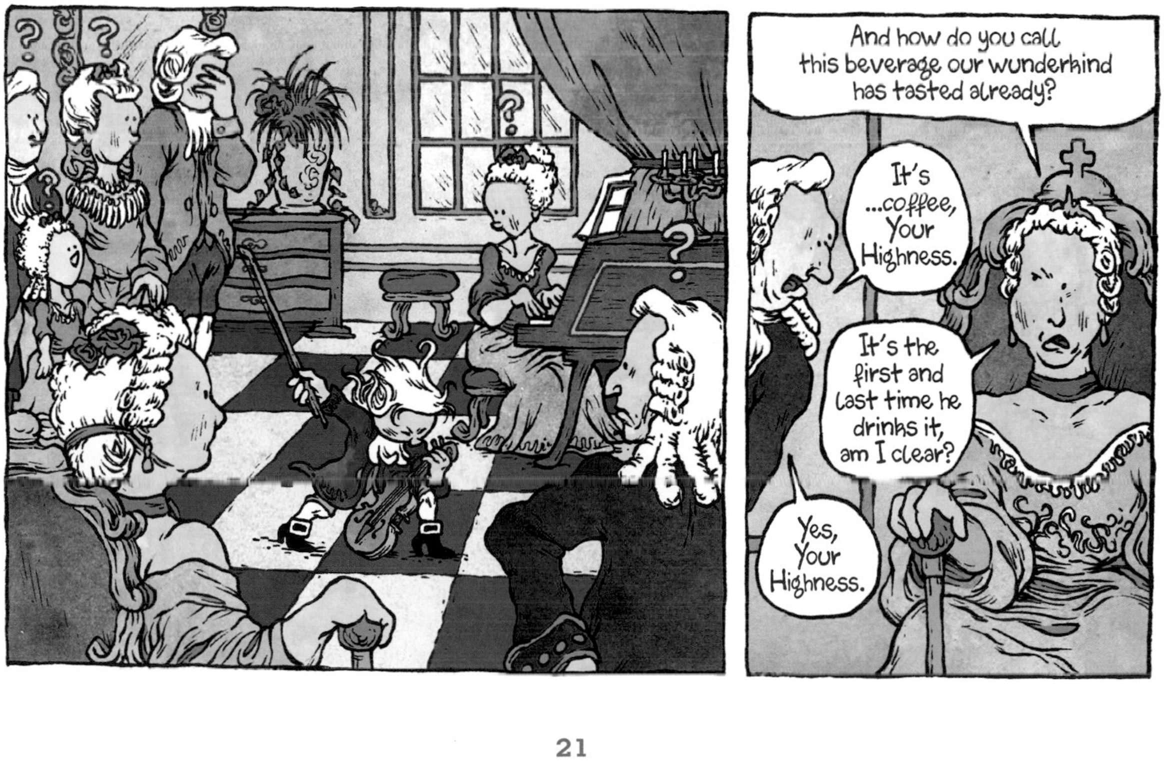

And how do you call this beverage our wunderkind has tasted already?
It's ...coffee, Your Highness.
It's the first and last time he drinks it, am I clear?
Yes, Your Highness.

The King of Instruments

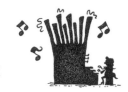

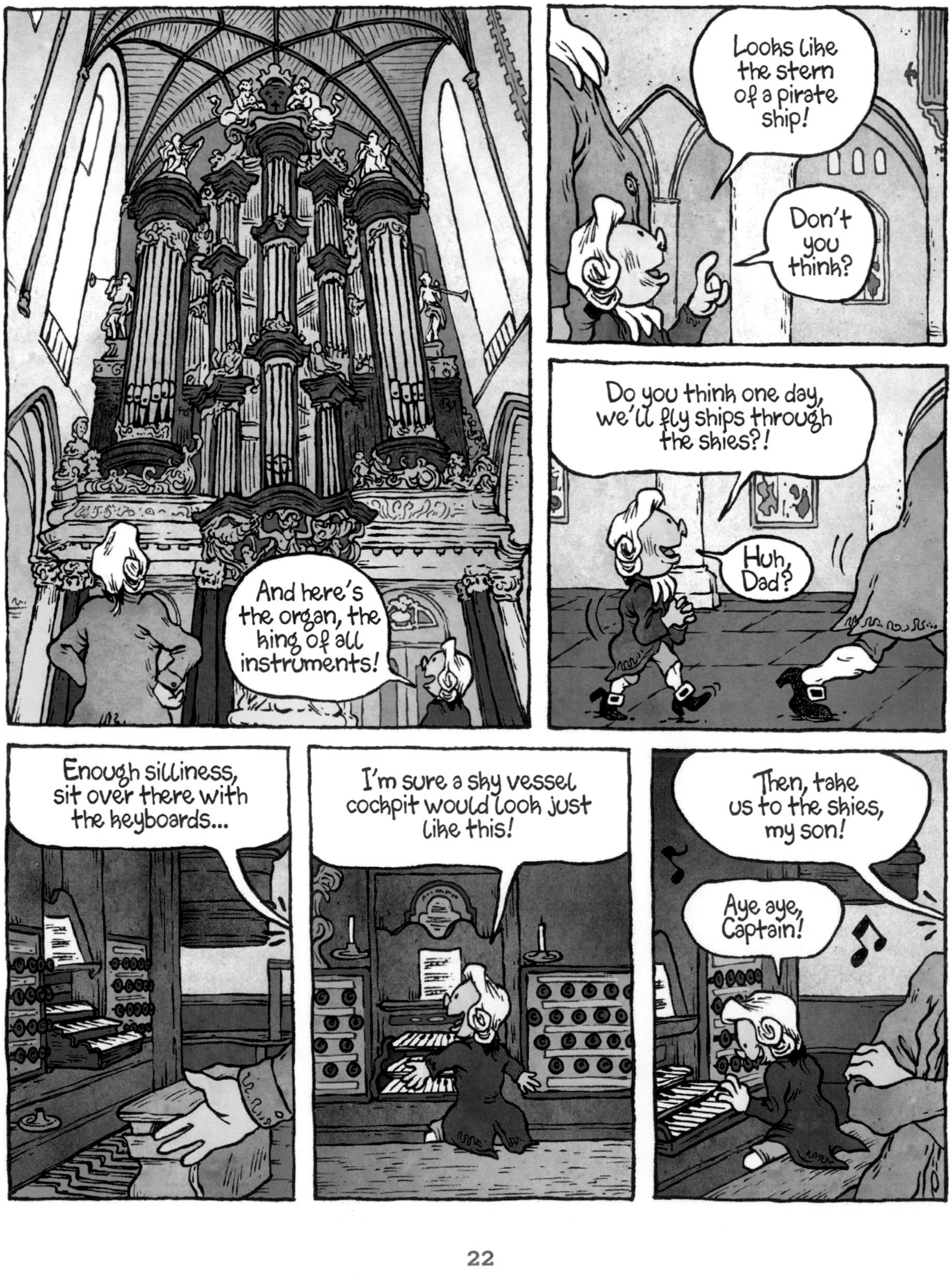
And here's the organ, the king of all instruments!
Looks like the stern of a pirate ship!
Don't you think?
Do you think one day, we'll fly ships through the skies?!
Huh, Dad?
Enough silliness, sit over there with the keyboards...
I'm sure a sky vessel cockpit would look just like this!
Then, take us to the skies, my son!
Aye aye, Captain!

Carnaval

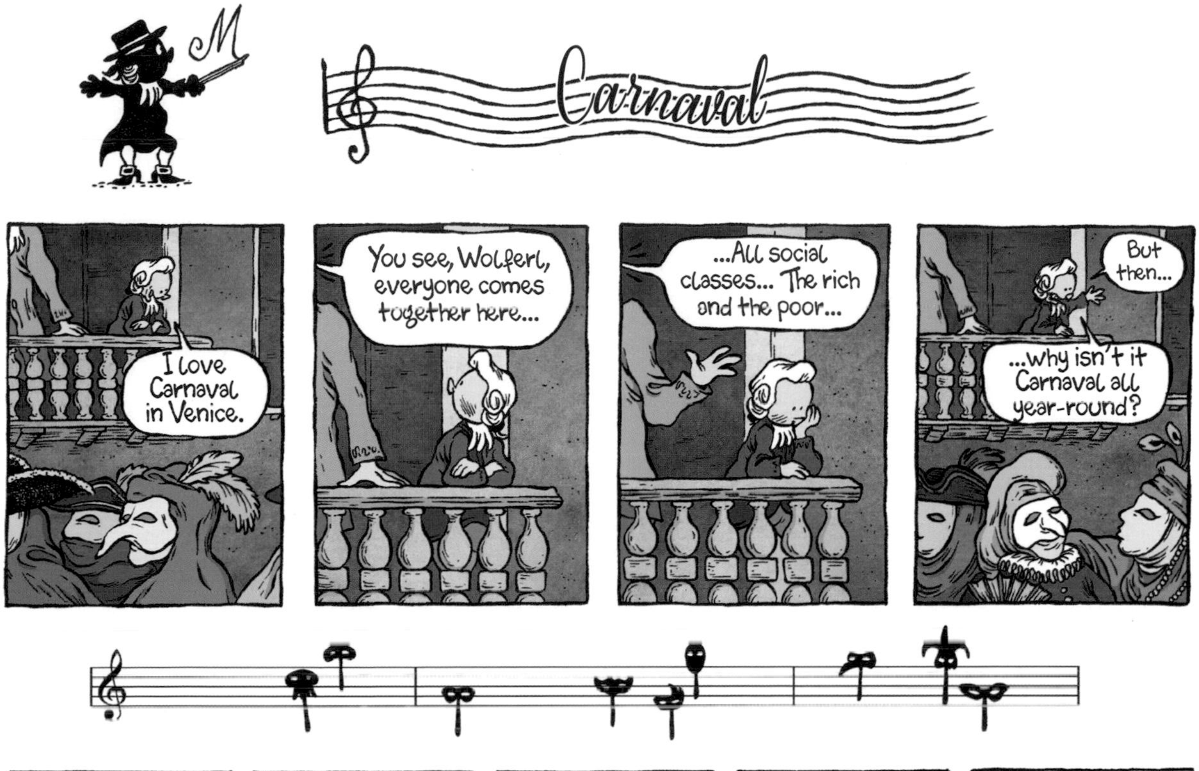
I love Carnaval in Venice.
You see, Wolferl, everyone comes together here...
...All social classes... The rich and the poor...
But then...
...why isn't it Carnaval all year-round?

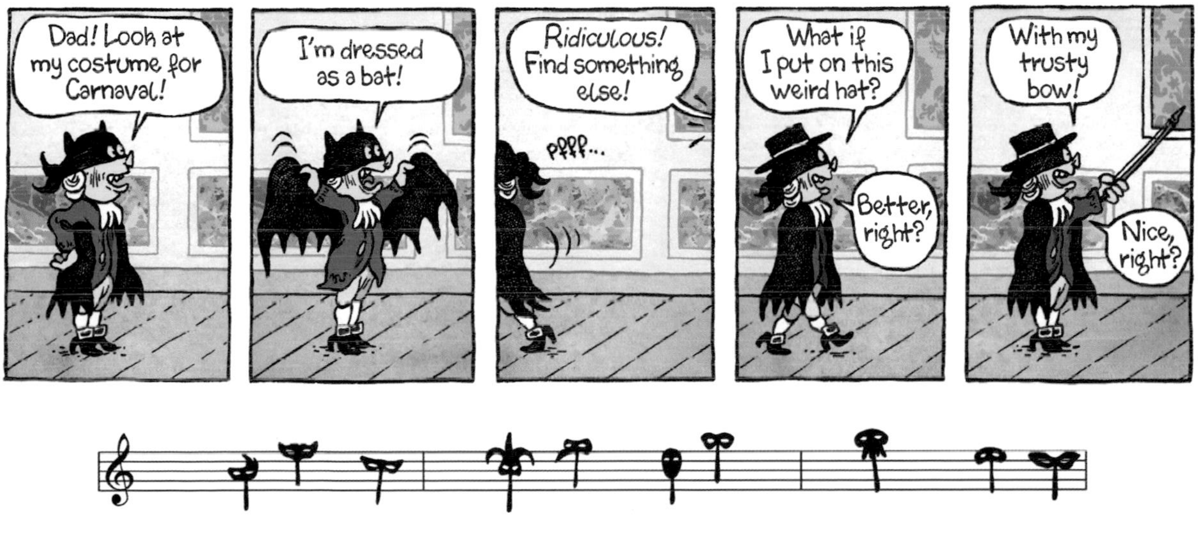
Dad! Look at my costume for Carnaval!
I'm dressed as a bat!
Ridiculous! Find something else!
pfff...
What if I put on this weird hat?
Better, right?
With my trusty bow!
Nice, right?

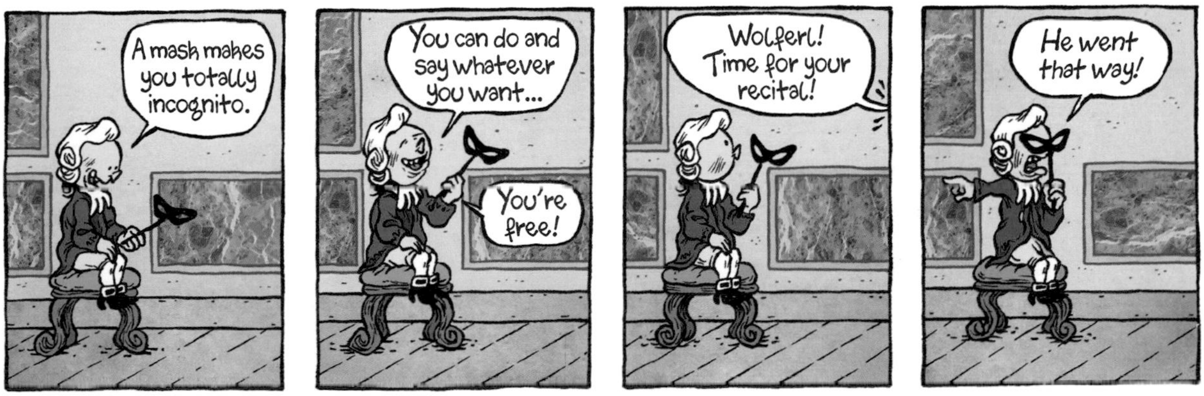
A mask makes you totally incognito.
You can do and say whatever you want...
You're free!
Wolferl! Time for your recital!
He went that way!

Pimberl

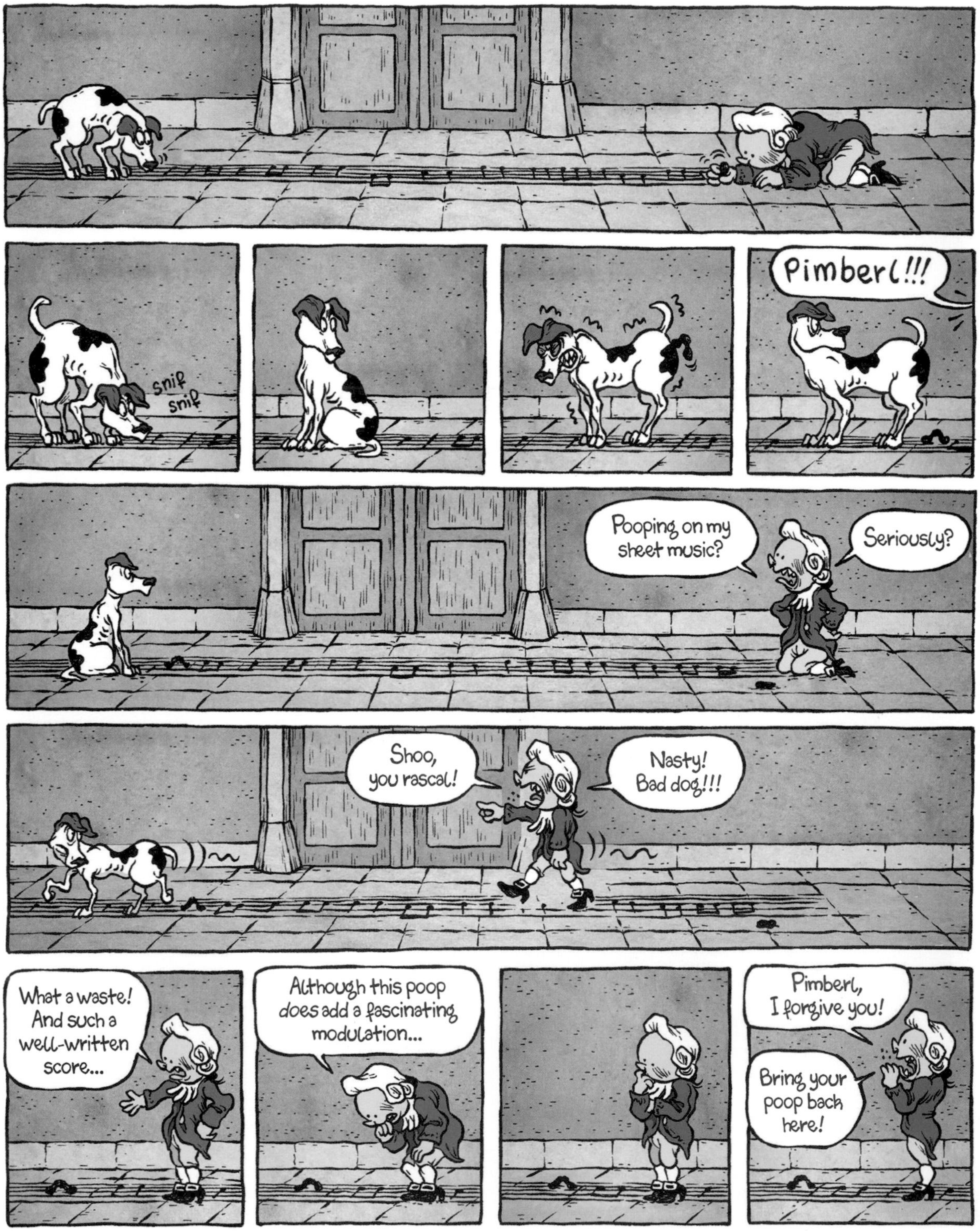
snif
snif
Pimberl!!!
Pooping on my sheet music?
Seriously?
Shoo, you rascal!
Nasty! Bad dog!!!
What a waste! And such a well-written score...
Although this poop *does* add a fascinating modulation...
Pimberl, I forgive you!
Bring your poop back here!

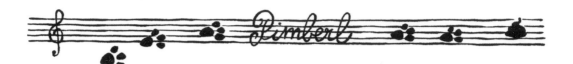

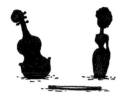

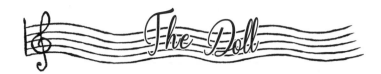

The Doll

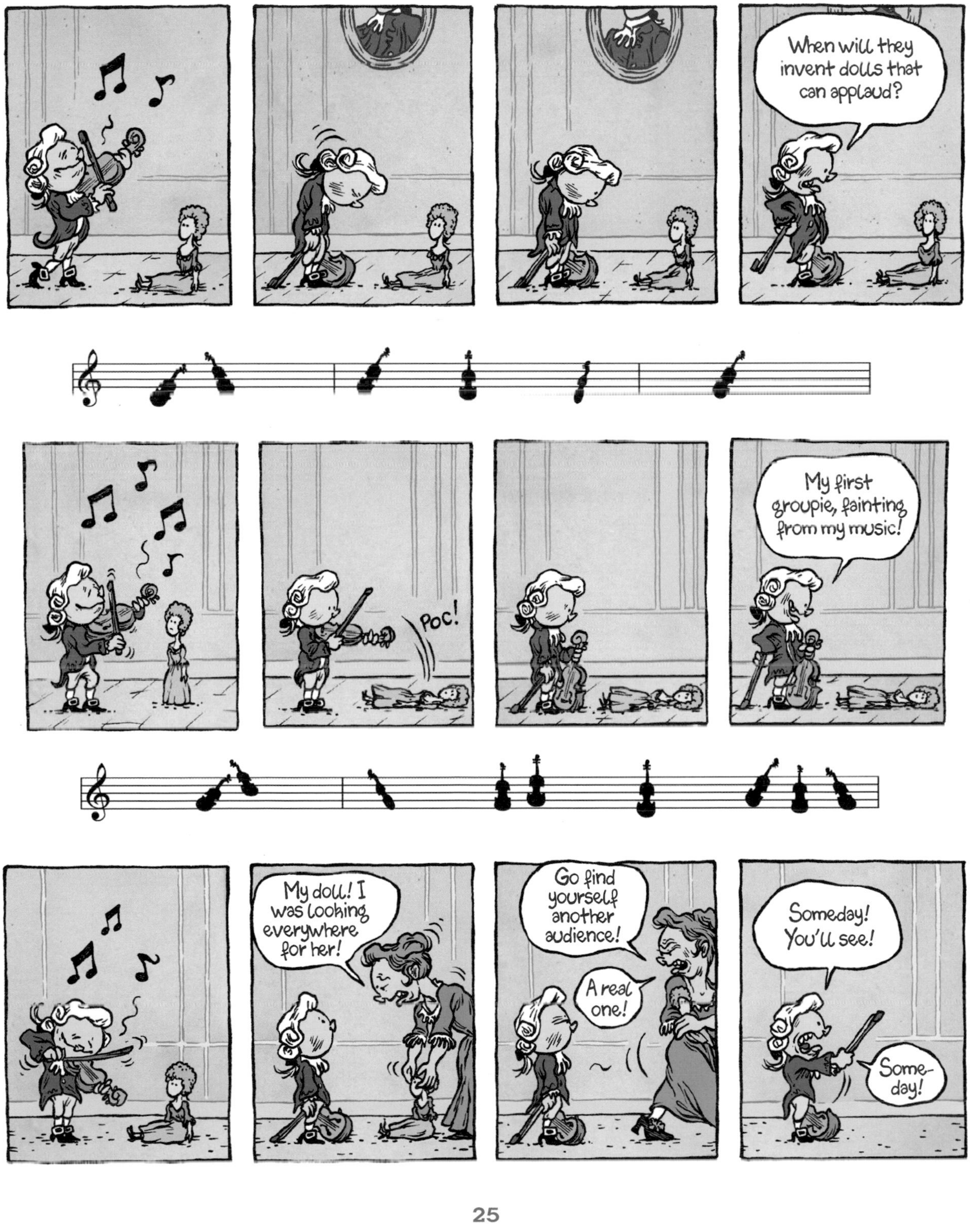
When will they invent dolls that can applaud?
POC!
My first groupie, fainting from my music!
My doll! I was looking everywhere for her!
Go find yourself another audience!
A real one!
Someday! You'll see!
Some-day!

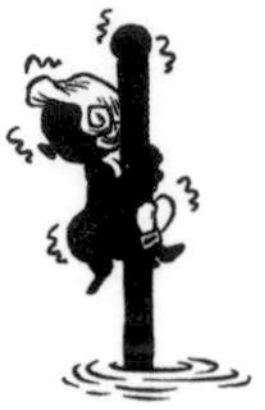

Aquaphobia

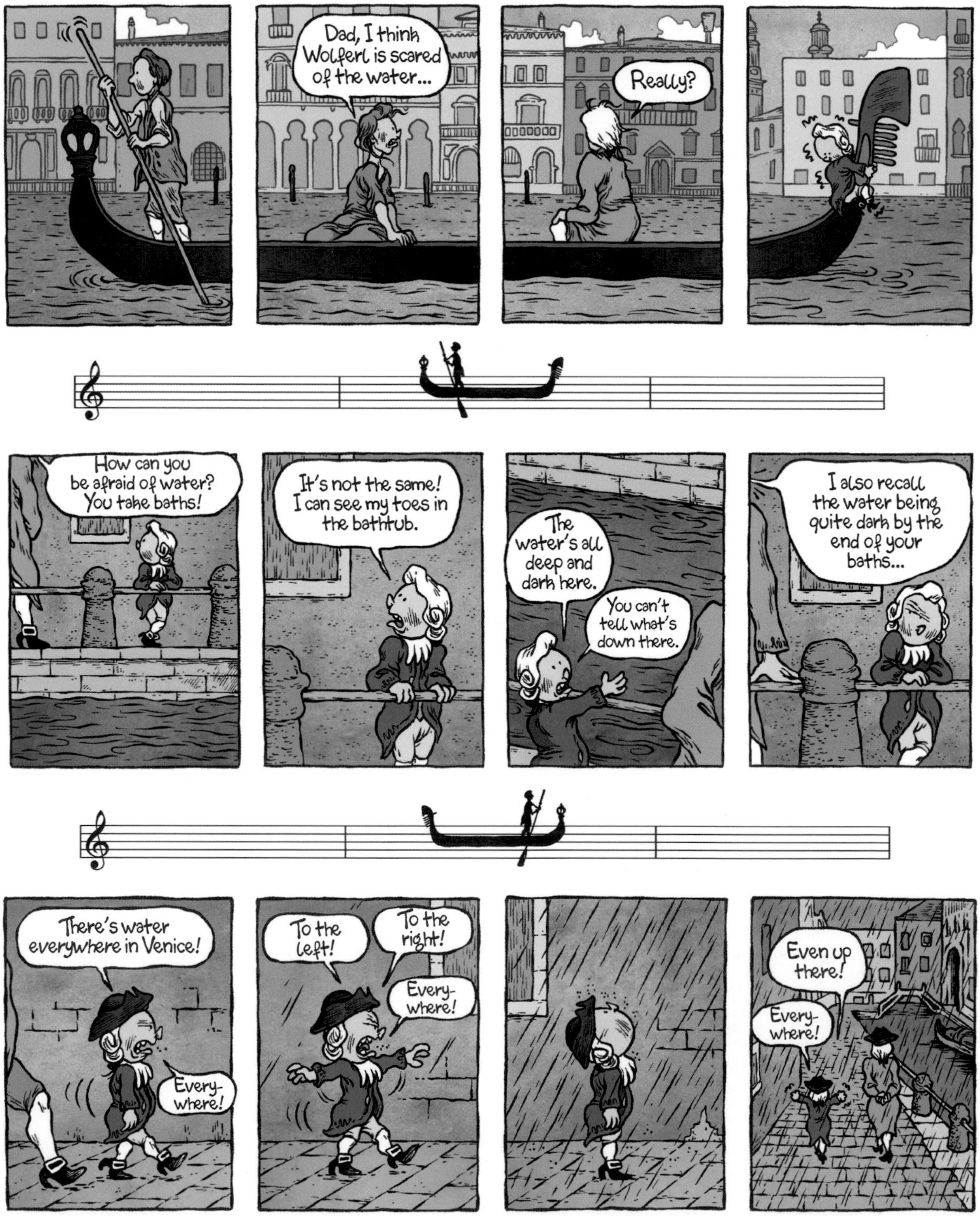

Dad, I think Wolferl is scared of the water...
Really?
How can you be afraid of water? You take baths!
It's not the same! I can see my toes in the bathtub.
The water's all deep and dark here.
You can't tell what's down there.
I also recall the water being quite dark by the end of your baths...
There's water everywhere in Venice!
Every-where!
To the left!
To the right!
Every-where!
Even up there!
Every-where!

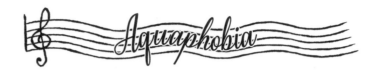

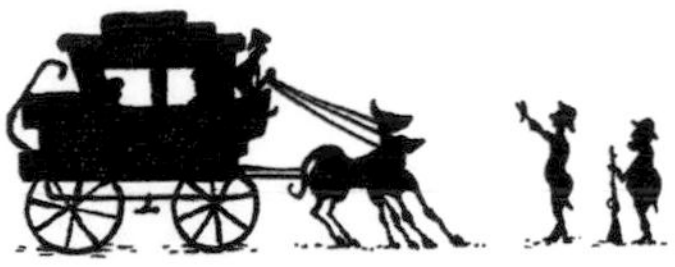

Halt!

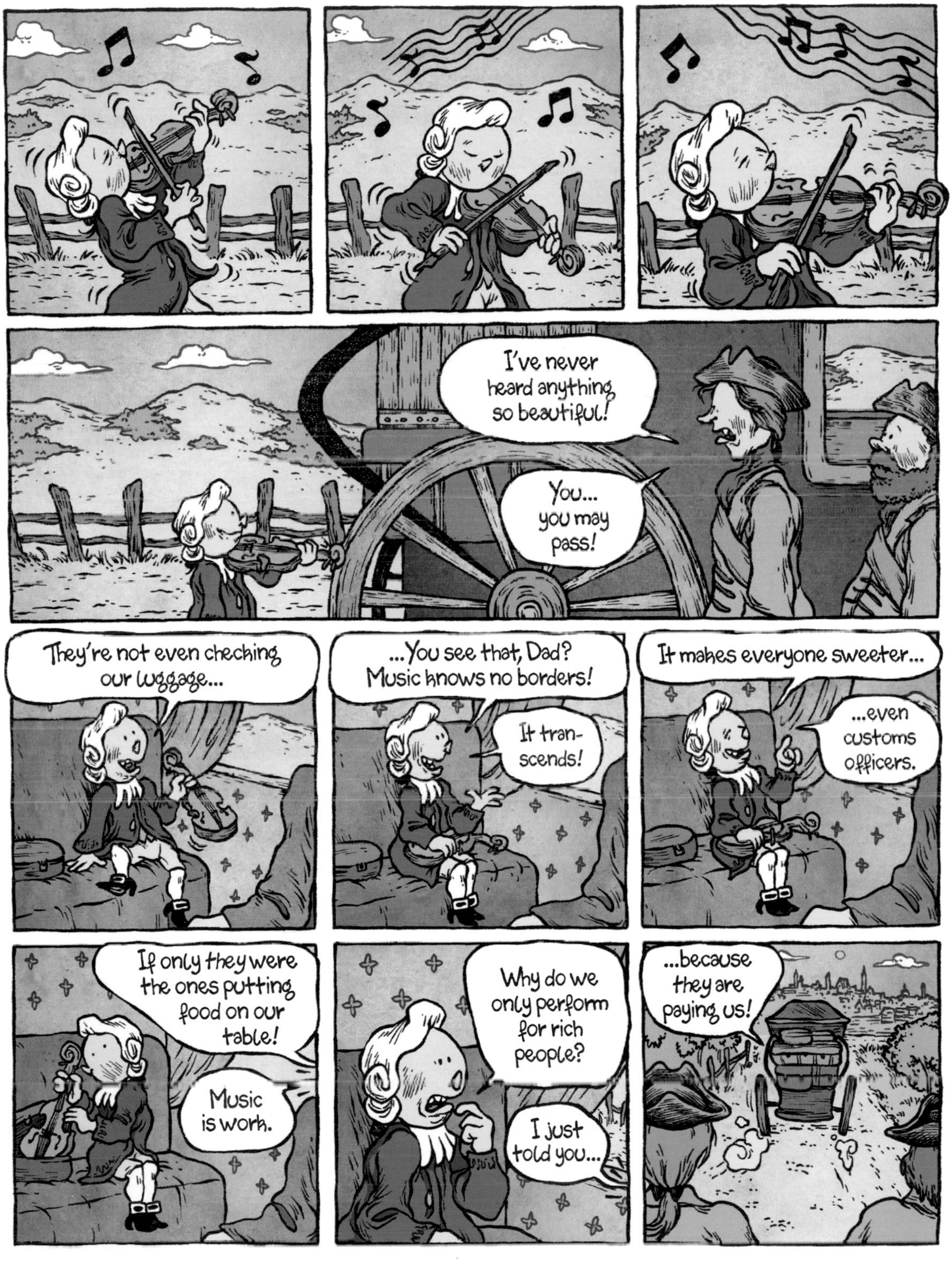

I've never heard anything so beautiful!
You... you may pass!
They're not even checking our luggage...
...You see that, Dad? Music knows no borders!
It tran-scends!
It makes everyone sweeter...
...even customs officers.
If only they were the ones putting food on our table!
Music is work.
Why do we only perform for rich people?
I just told you...
...because they are paying us!

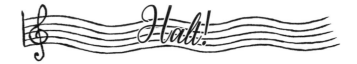

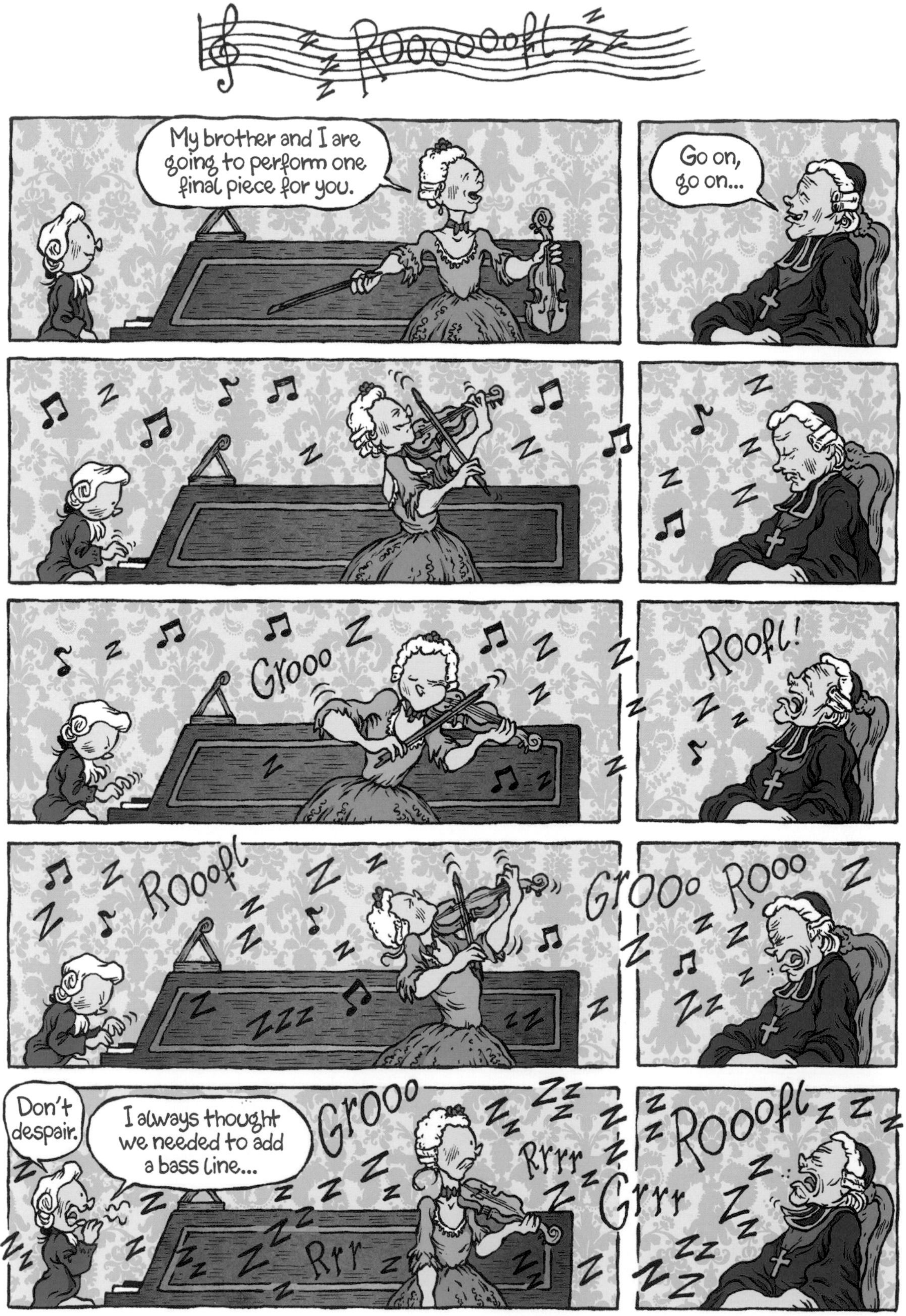

Roooooofl
My brother and I are going to perform one final piece for you.
Go on, go on...
Grooo
Roofl!
Rooofl
Grooo
Rooo
Don't despair.
I always thought we needed to add a bass line...
Grooo
Rrrr
Rrr
Grrr
Rooofl

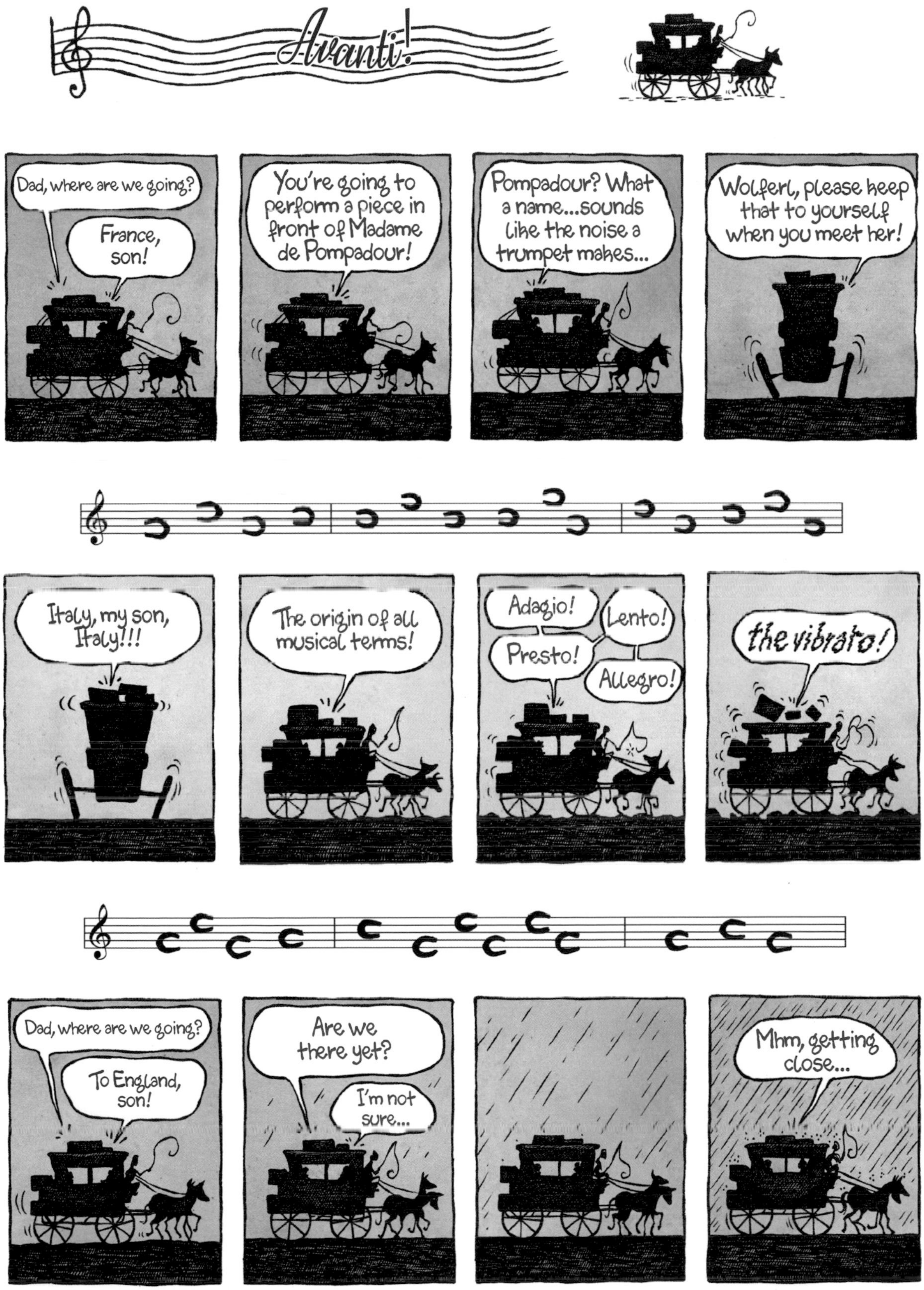
Avanti!
Dad, where are we going?
France, son!
You're going to perform a piece in front of Madame de Pompadour!
Pompadour? What a name...sounds like the noise a trumpet makes...
Wolferl, please keep that to yourself when you meet her!
Italy, my son, Italy!!!
The origin of all musical terms!
Adagio!
Lento!
Presto!
Allegro!
the vibrato!
Dad, where are we going?
To England, son!
Are we there yet?
I'm not sure...
Mhm, getting close...

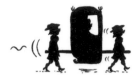

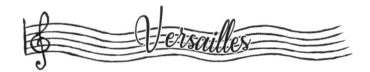

Versailles

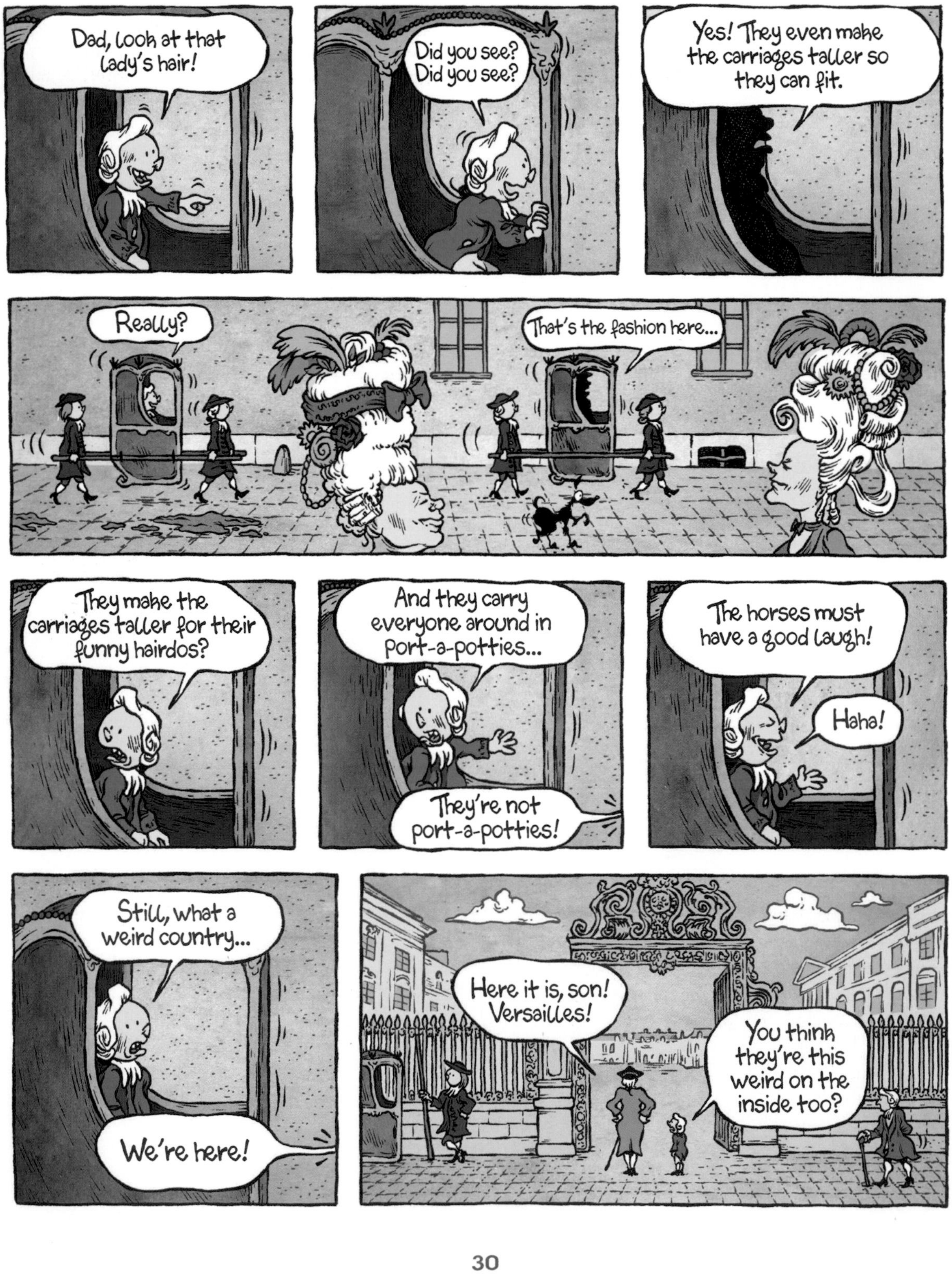

Dad, look at that lady's hair!
Did you see? Did you see?
Yes! They even make the carriages taller so they can fit.
Really?
That's the fashion here...
They make the carriages taller for their funny hairdos?
And they carry everyone around in port-a-potties...
They're not port-a-potties!
The horses must have a good laugh!
Haha!
Still, what a weird country...
We're here!
Here it is, son! Versailles!
You think they're this weird on the inside too?

Nannerl

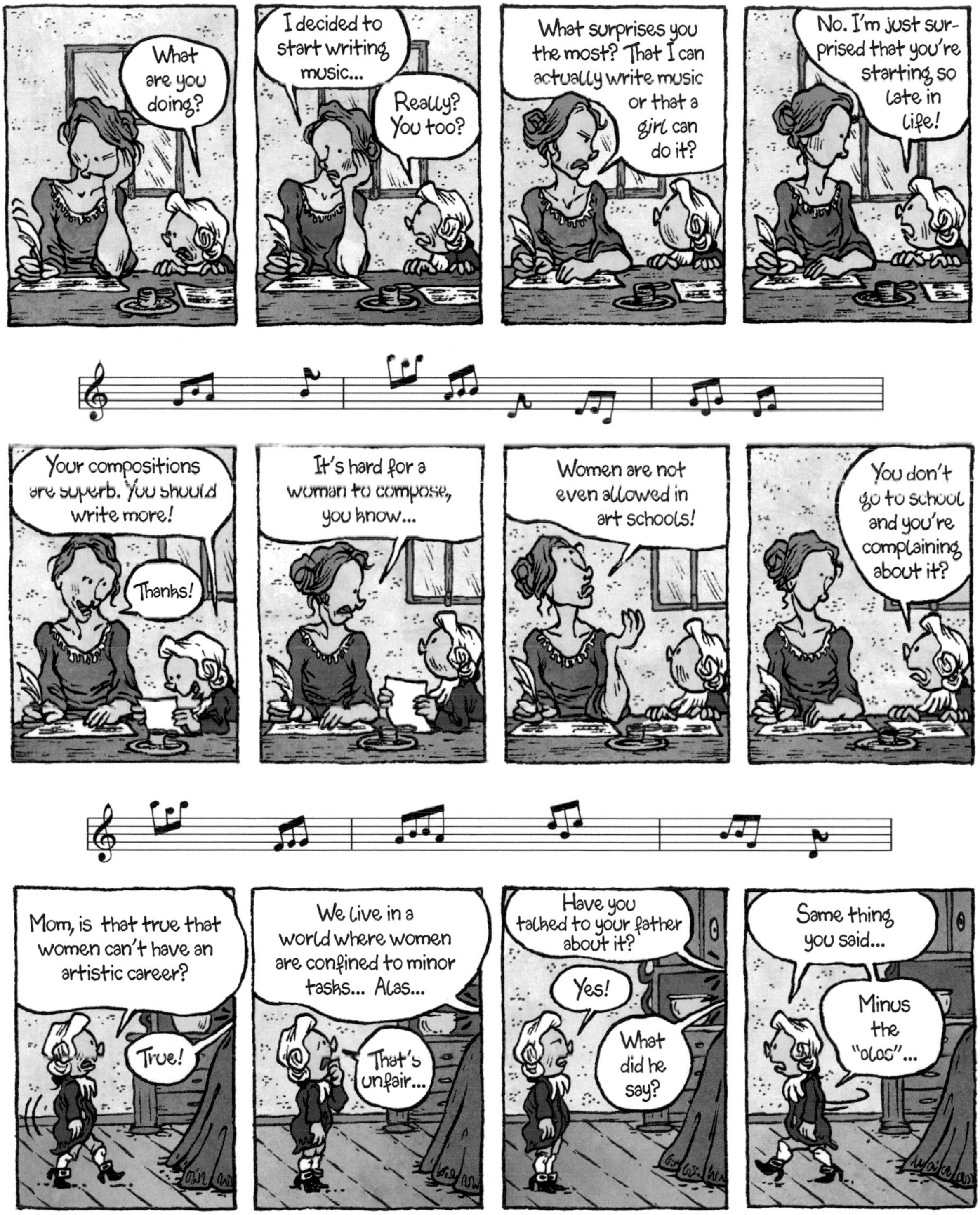

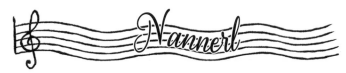

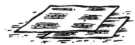

What are you doing?
I decided to start writing music...
Really? You too?
What surprises you the most? That I can actually write music or that a girl can do it?
No. I'm just surprised that you're starting so late in life!
Your compositions are superb. You should write more!
Thanks!
It's hard for a woman to compose, you know...
Women are not even allowed in art schools!
You don't go to school and you're complaining about it?
Mom, is that true that women can't have an artistic career?
True!
We live in a world where women are confined to minor tasks... Alas...
That's unfair...
Have you talked to your father about it?
Yes!
What did he say?
Same thing you said...
Minus the "alas"...

Blub Blub
Mom, I don't have time for a bath!
I have to compose!
After your bath! Now take off your wig!
Are you suggesting that I take a bath totally naked?!
Blo Blop Bloo Bloo Blo Blo Blop
Wolferl! Stop making those disgusting sounds!
Disgusting sounds?
You mean my bathing music??
What an idea! I'll put the bathtub in front of my harpsichord...
Now I can wash myself and play at the same time!
I'm a genius!
Wolferl! Where's the bathtub?
gnn...
I hope it's not in front of the harpsichord!
Can't reach...

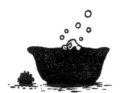

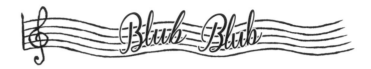

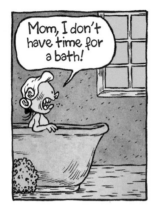

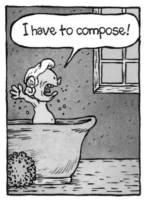

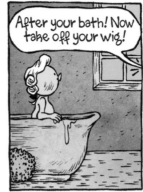

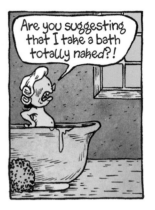

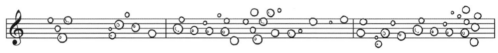

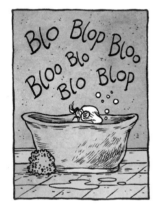

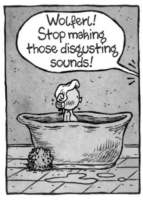

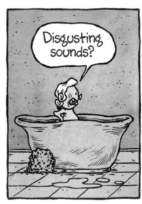

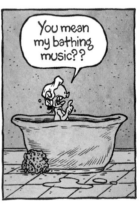

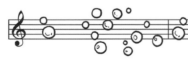

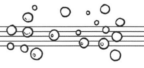

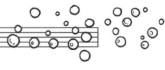

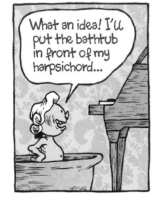

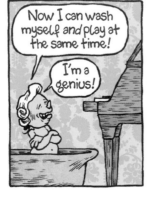

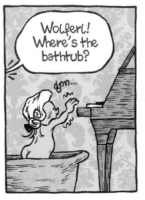

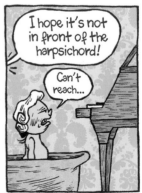

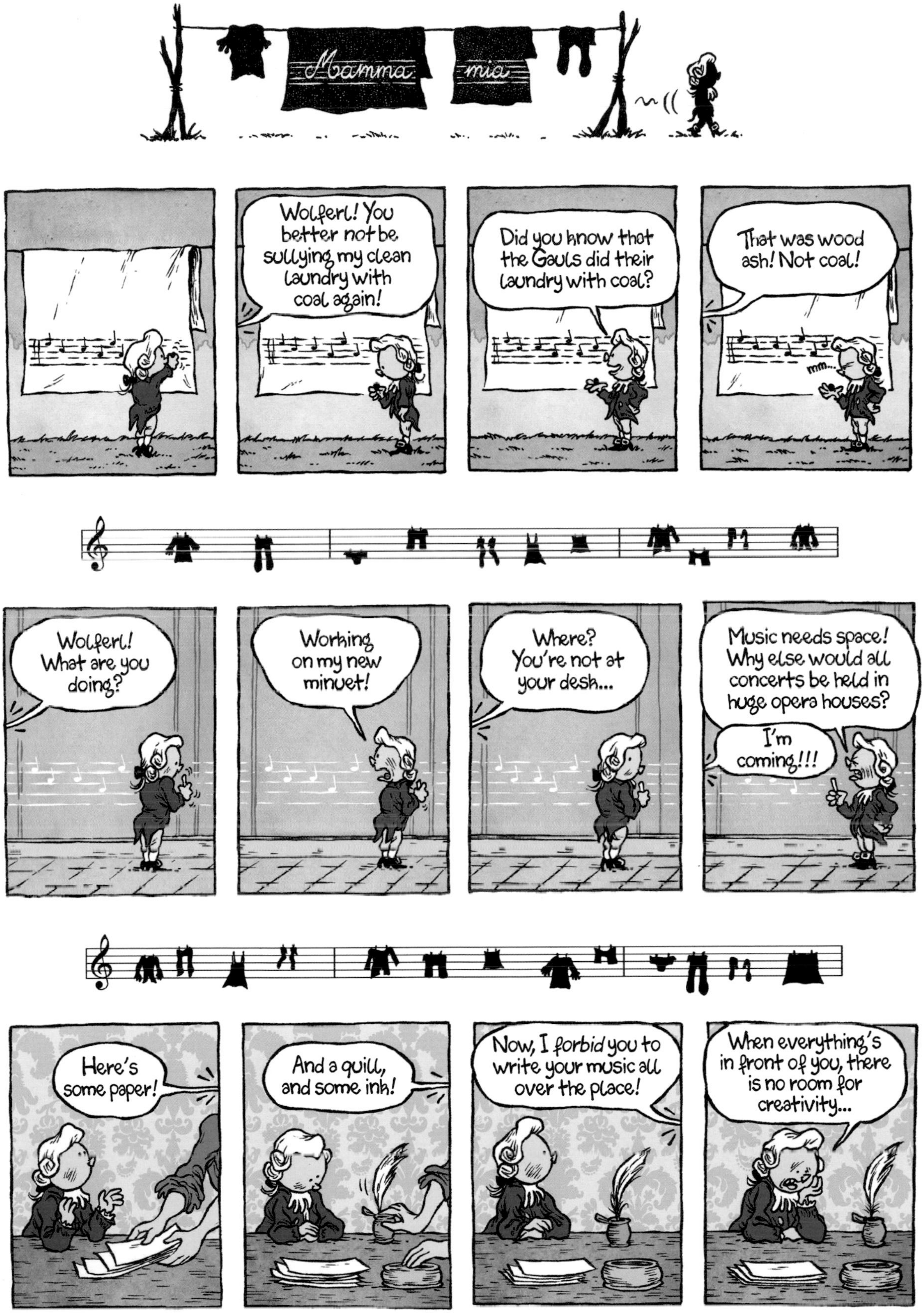
Mamma mia
Wolferl! You better not be sullying my clean laundry with coal again!
Did you know that the Gauls did their laundry with coal?
That was wood ash! Not coal!
mm...
Wolferl! What are you doing?
Working on my new minuet!
Where? You're not at your desk...
Music needs space! Why else would all concerts be held in huge opera houses?
I'm coming!!!
Here's some paper!
And a quill, and some ink!
Now, I *forbid* you to write your music all over the place!
When everything's in front of you, there is no room for creativity...

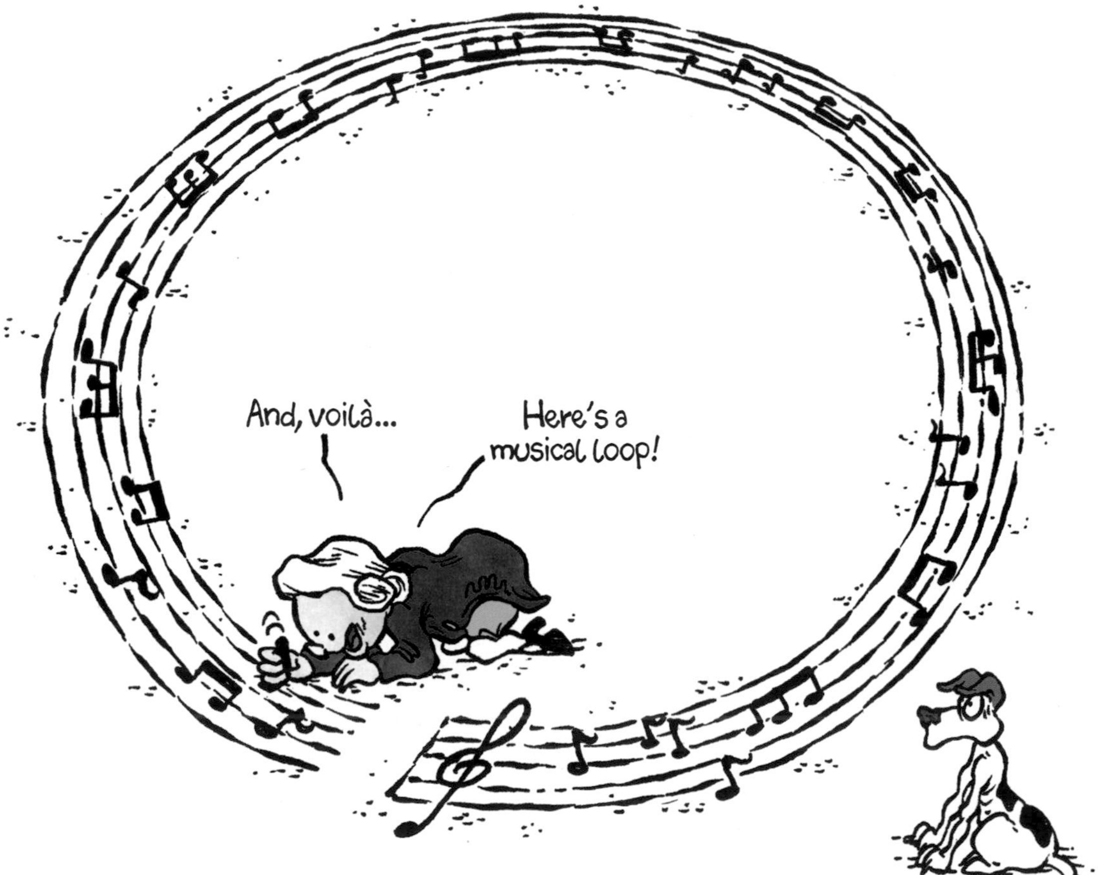
And, voilà...
Here's a musical loop!

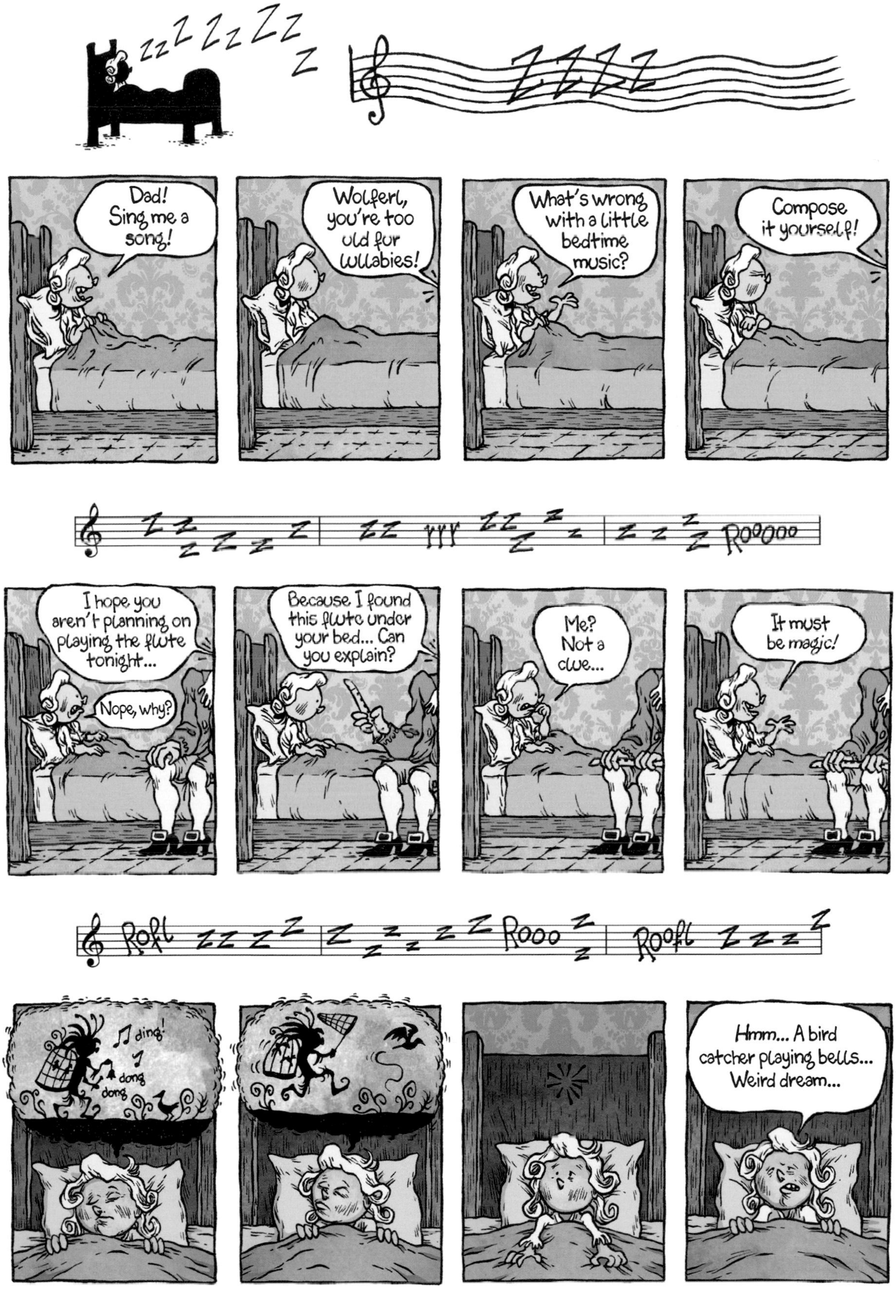
zzZZzZZz Z
ZZZZ
Dad! Sing me a song!
Wolferl, you're too old for lullabies!
What's wrong with a little bedtime music?
Compose it yourself!
zz zz z z z zz yyy zz z z z z z z z Roeooo
I hope you aren't planning on playing the flute tonight...
Nope, why?
Because I found this flute under your bed... Can you explain?
Me? Not a clue...
It must be magic!
Rofl zzzz z z z z z z z Rooo z z Roofl z z z z
ding!
dong
dong
Hmm... A bird catcher playing bells... Weird dream...

The Little Birdie

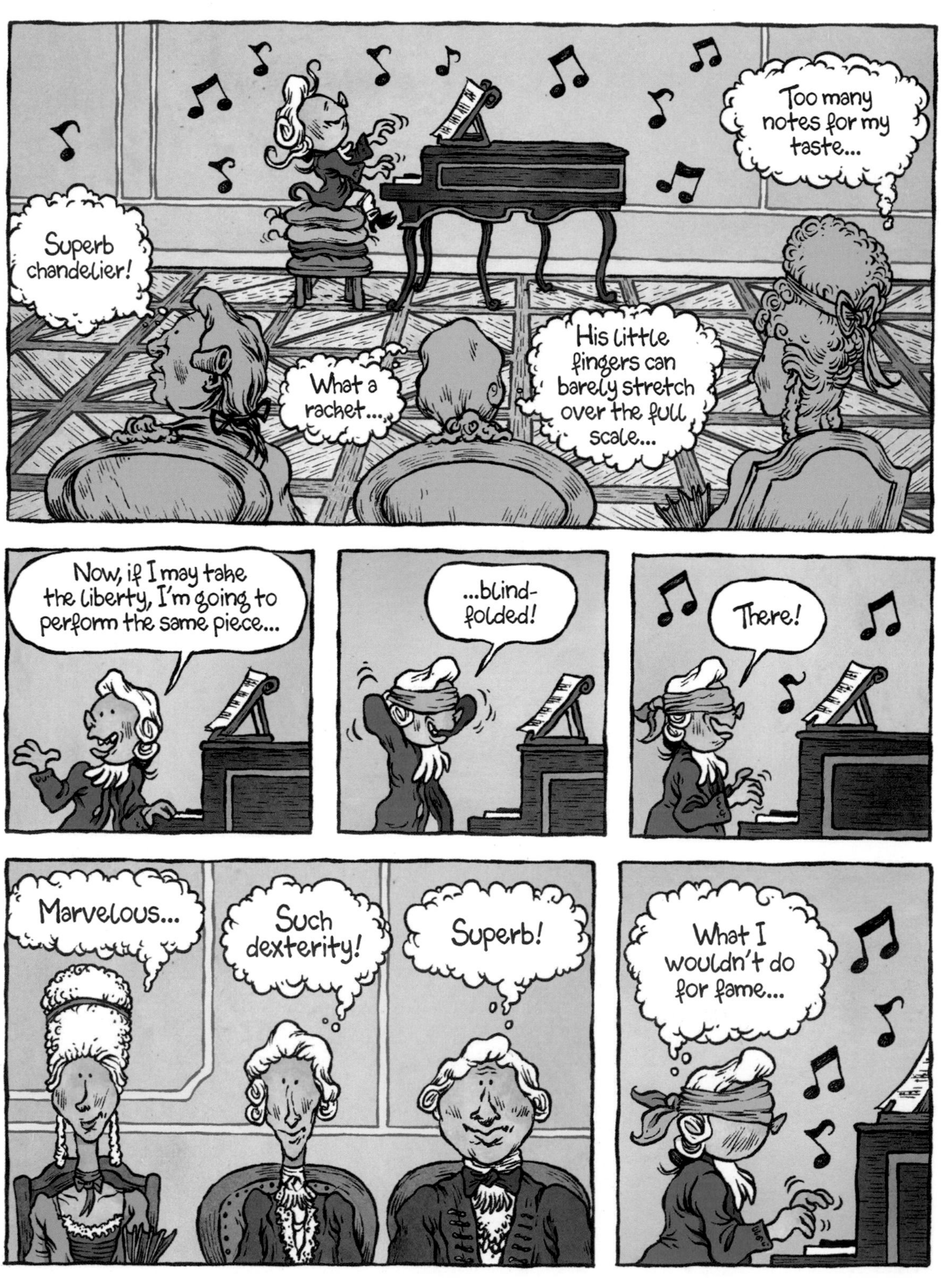
Superb chandelier!
What a racket...
His little fingers can barely stretch over the full scale...
Too many notes for my taste...
Now, if I may take the liberty, I'm going to perform the same piece...
...blind-folded!
There!
Marvelous...
Such dexterity!
Superb!
What I wouldn't do for fame...

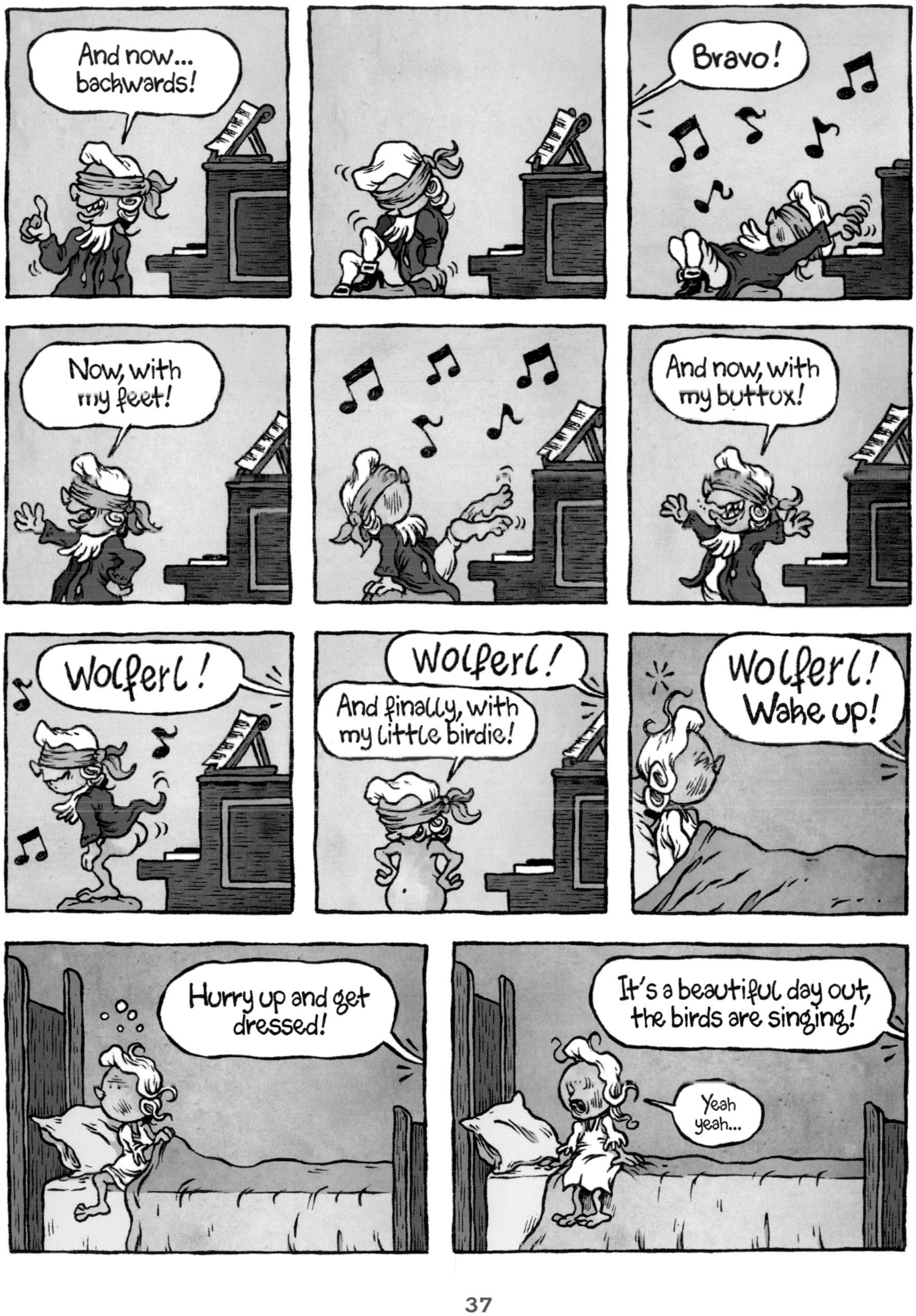

And now... backwards!
Bravo!
Now, with my feet!
And now, with my buttox!
Wolferl!
Wolferl!
And finally, with my little birdie!
Wolferl! Wake up!
Hurry up and get dressed!
It's a beautiful day out, the birds are singing!
Yeah yeah...

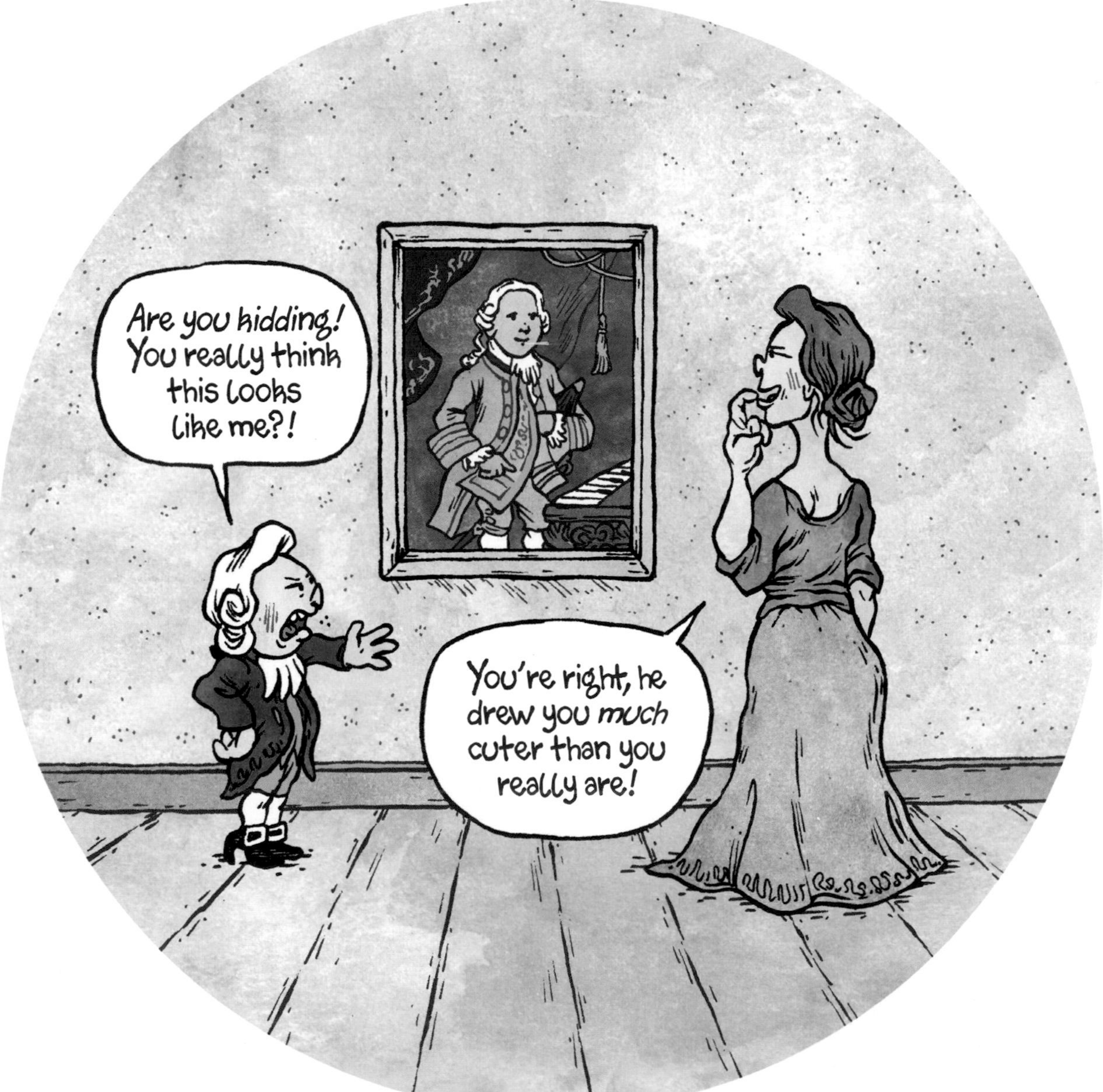
Are you kidding! You really think this looks like me?!
You're right, he drew you *much* cuter than you really are!

Medusa

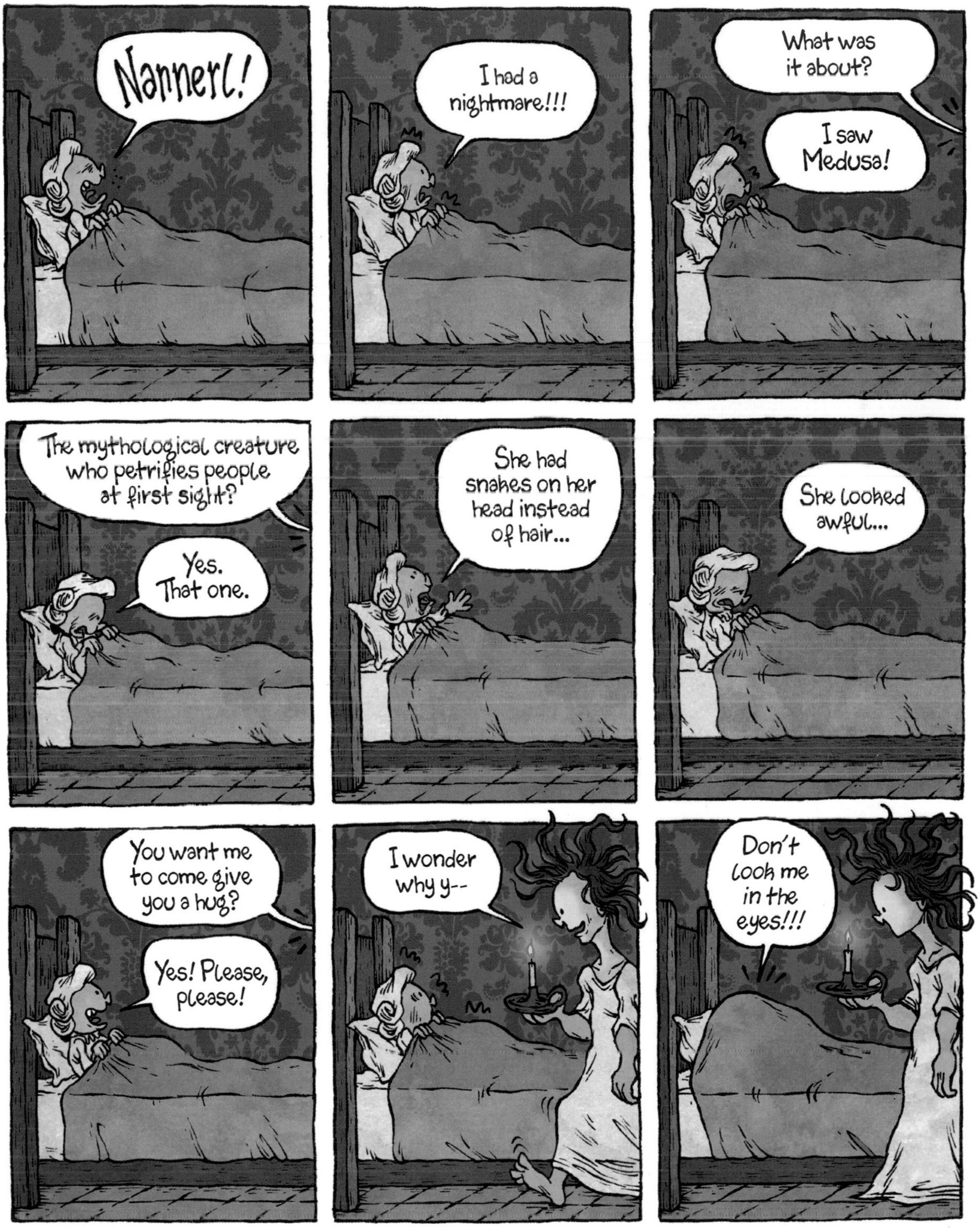

Nannerl!
I had a nightmare!!!
What was it about?
I saw Medusa!
The mythological creature who petrifies people at first sight?
Yes. That one.
She had snakes on her head instead of hair...
She looked awful...
You want me to come give you a hug?
Yes! Please, please!
I wonder why y--
Don't look me in the eyes!!!

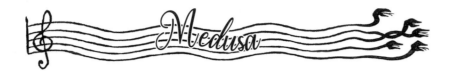

Scarlet Fever

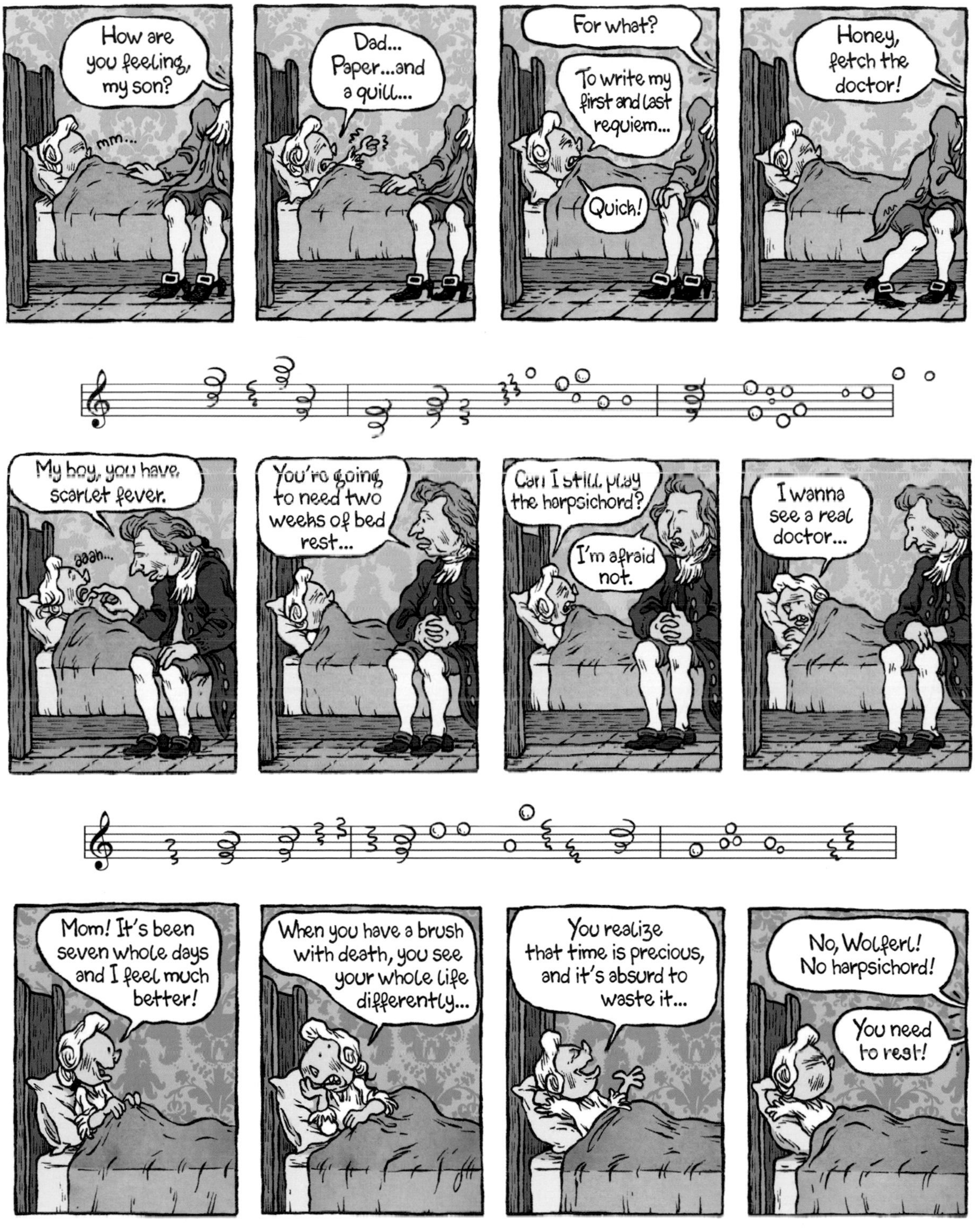

How are you feeling, my son?
mm...
Dad... Paper...and a quill...
For what?
To write my first and last requiem...
Quick!
Honey, fetch the doctor!
My boy, you have scarlet fever.
aaah...
You're going to need two weeks of bed rest...
Can I still play the harpsichord?
I'm afraid not.
I wanna see a real doctor...
Mom! It's been seven whole days and I feel much better!
When you have a brush with death, you see your whole life differently...
You realize that time is precious, and it's absurd to waste it...
No, Wolferl! No harpsichord!
You need to rest!

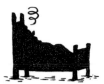

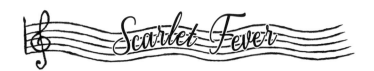

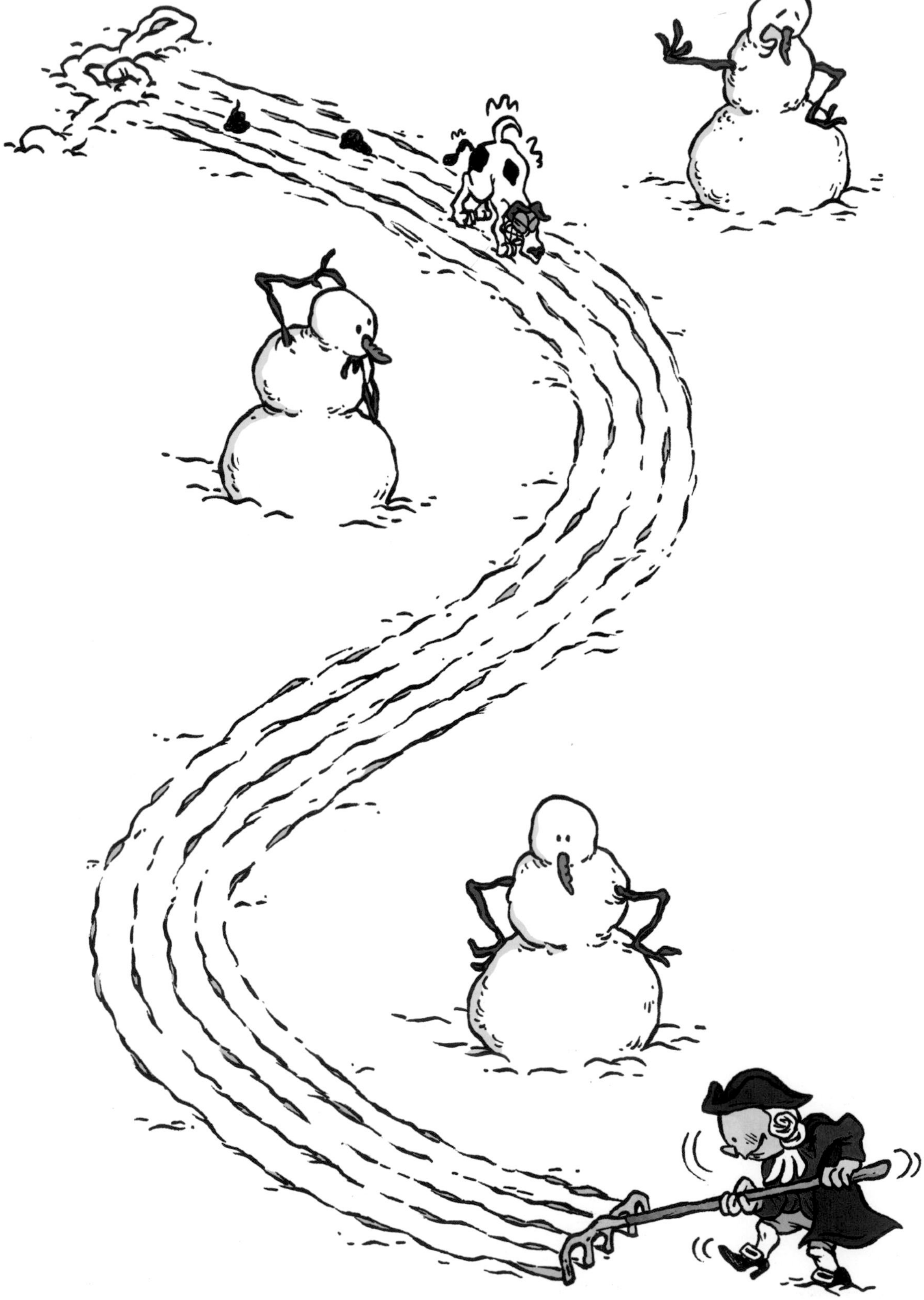

Bis Repetita Placent

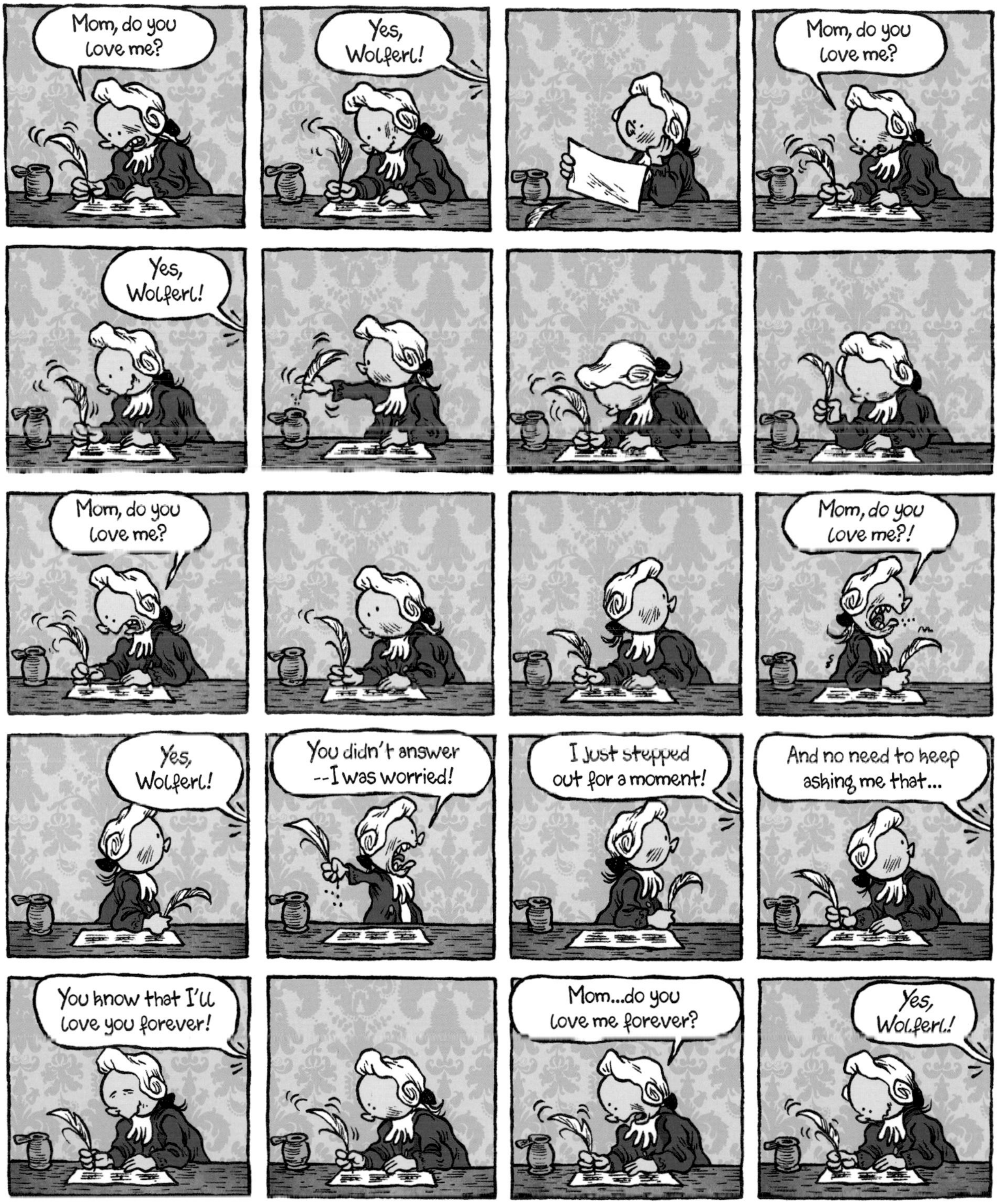

Mom, do you love me?
Yes, Wolferl!
Mom, do you love me?
Yes, Wolferl!
Mom, do you love me?
Mom, do you love me?!
Yes, Wolferl!
You didn't answer --I was worried!
I just stepped out for a moment!
And no need to keep asking me that...
You know that I'll love you forever!
Mom...do you love me forever?
Yes, Wolferl!

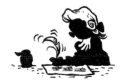

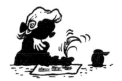

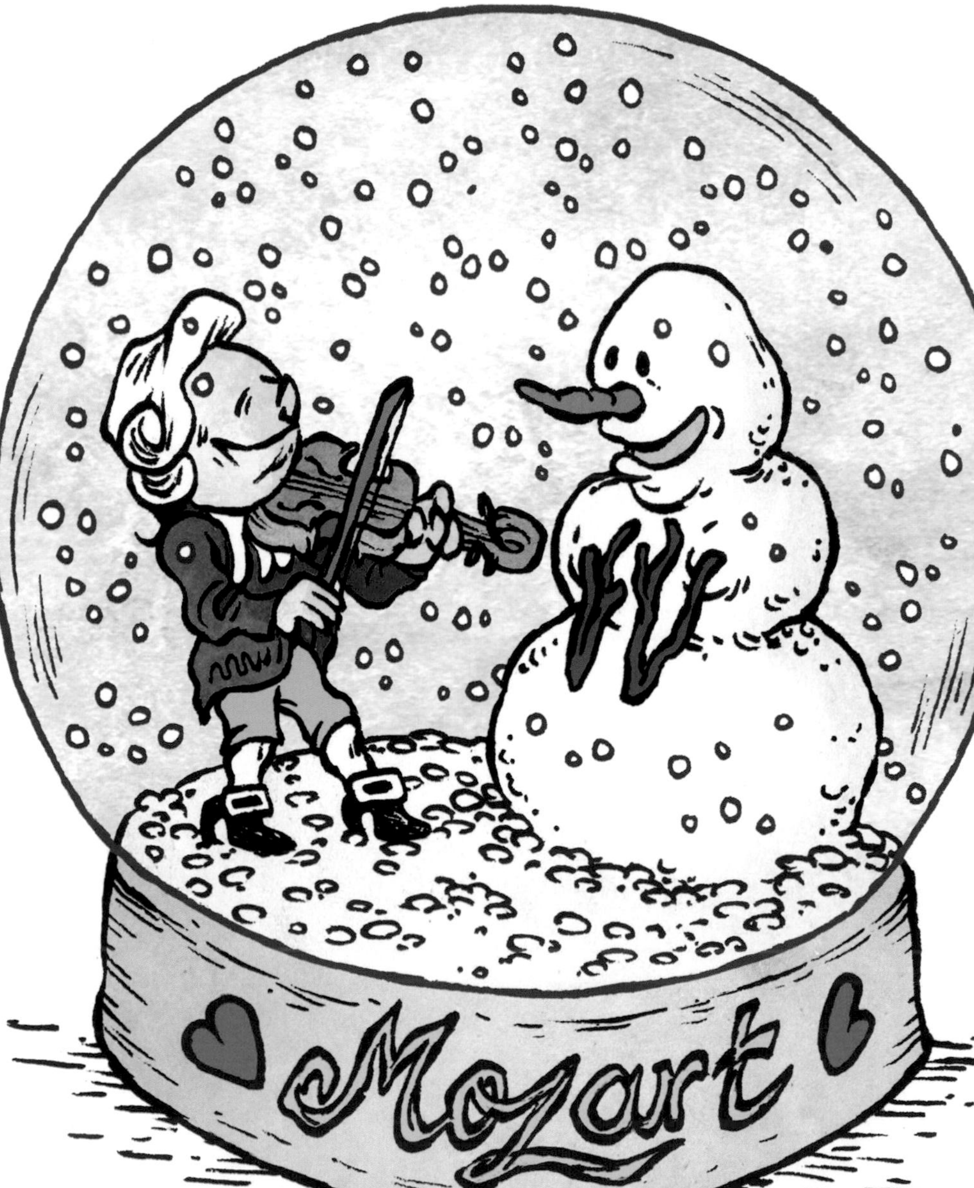
Mozart

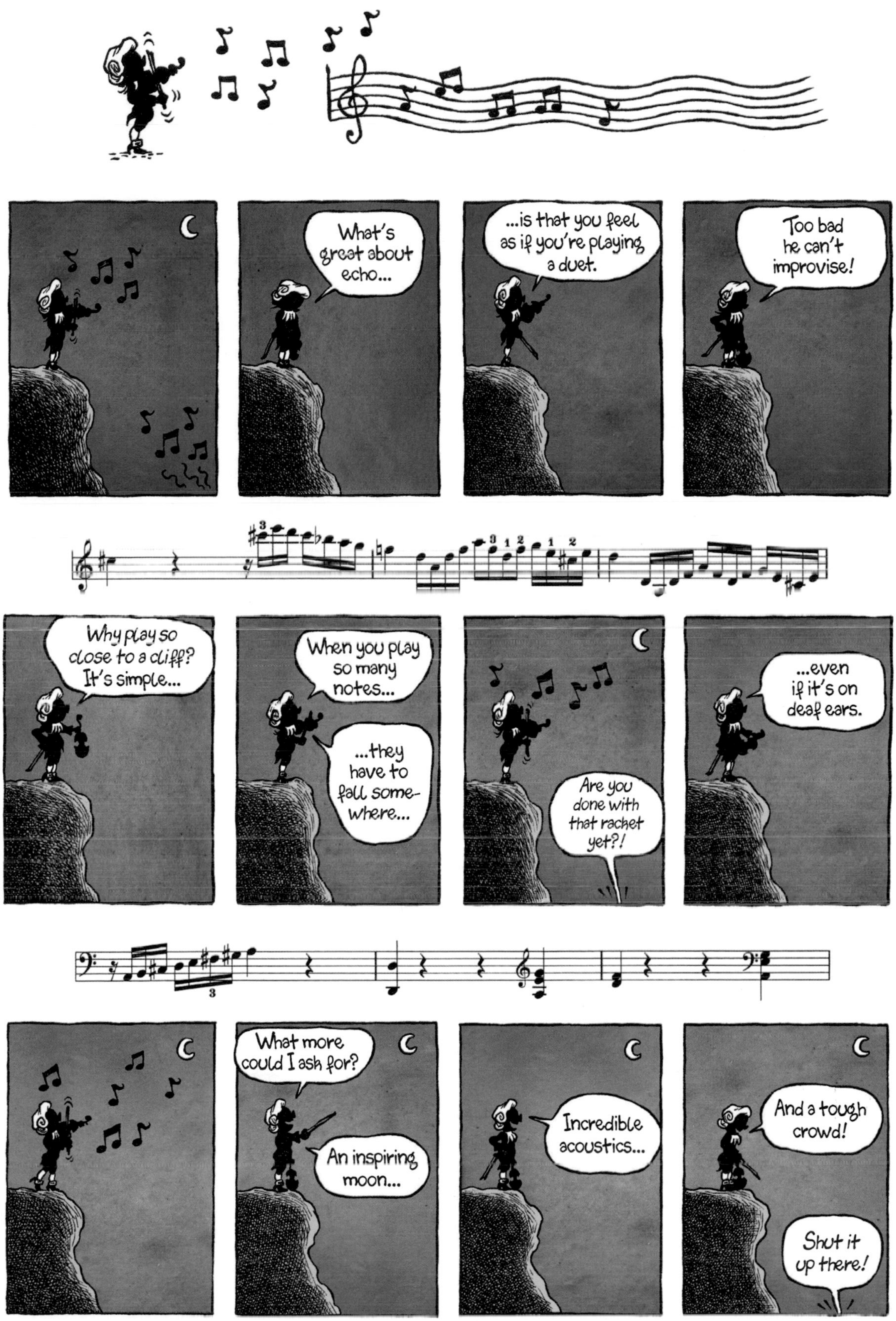
What's great about echo...
...is that you feel as if you're playing a duet.
Too bad he can't improvise!
Why play so close to a cliff? It's simple...
When you play so many notes...
...they have to fall some-where...
Are you done with that rachet yet?!
...even if it's on deaf ears.
What more could I ask for?
An inspiring moon...
Incredible acoustics...
And a tough crowd!
Shut it up there!

A Flaky Audience

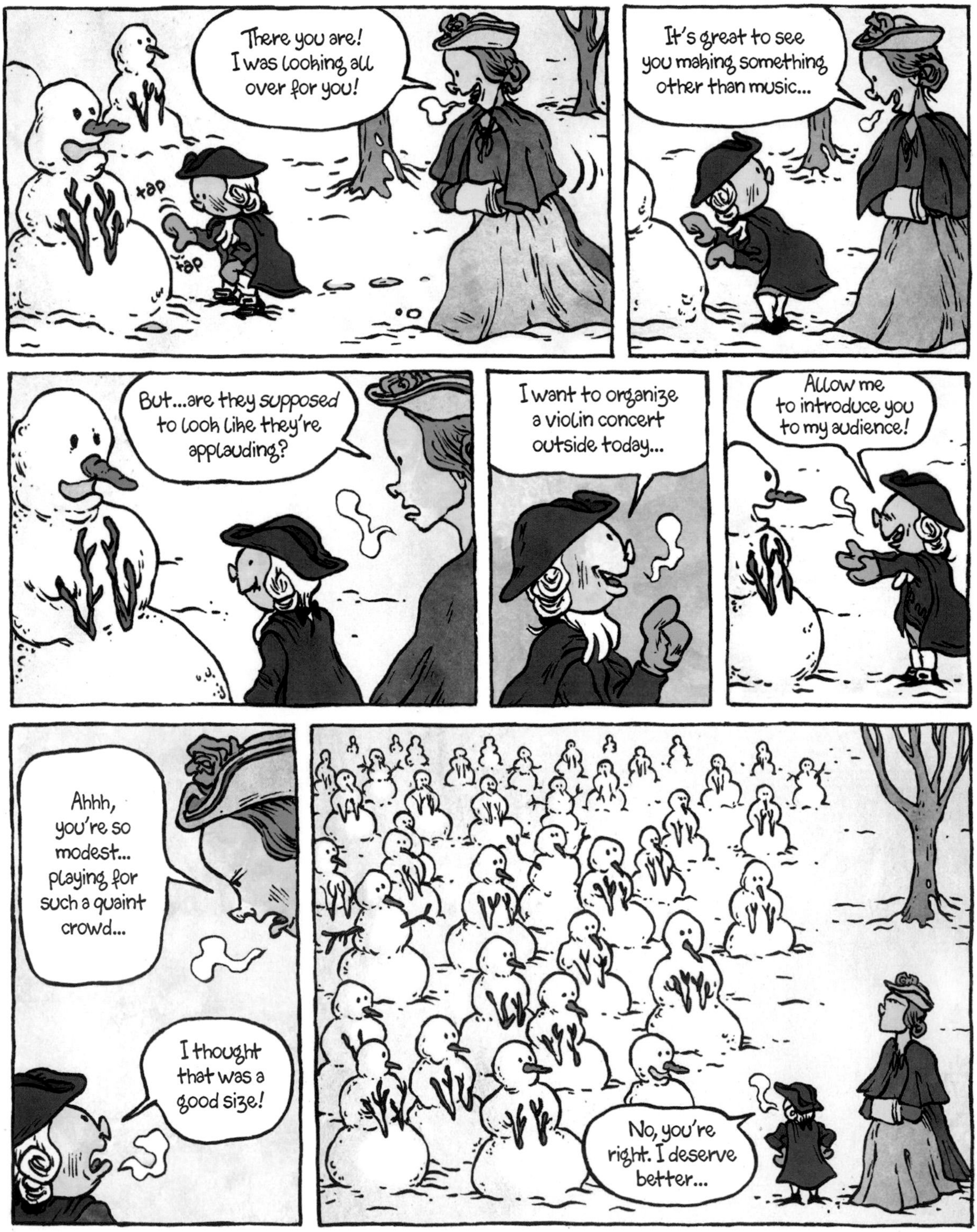
There you are! I was looking all over for you!
tap
tap
It's great to see you making something other than music...
But...are they *supposed* to look like they're applauding?
I want to organize a violin concert outside today...
Allow me to introduce you to my audience!
Ahhh, you're so modest... playing for such a quaint crowd...
I thought that was a good size!
No, you're right. I deserve better...

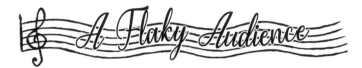

Canary Cry

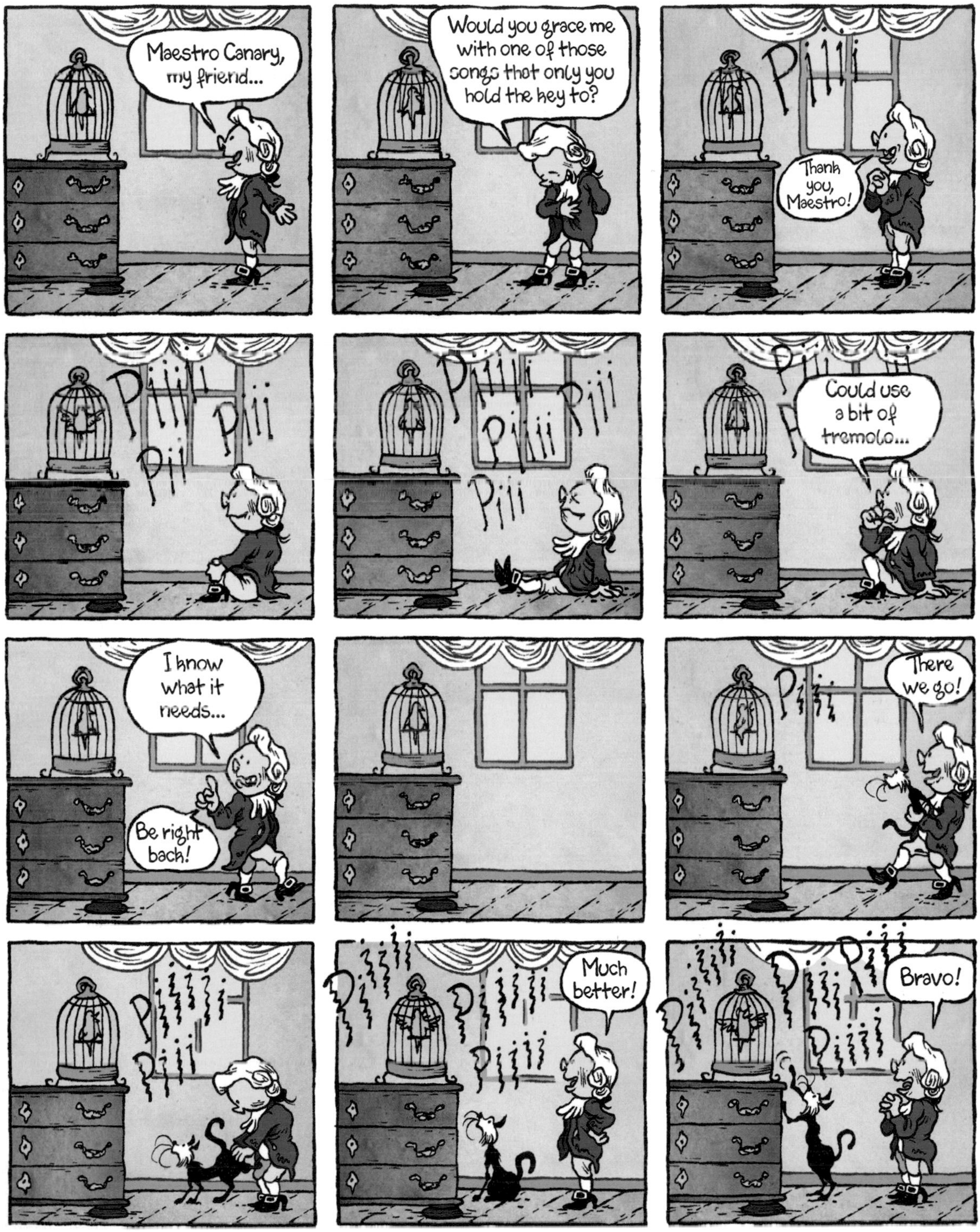
Maestro Canary, my friend...
Would you grace me with one of those songs that only you hold the key to?
Thank you, Maestro!
Could use a bit of tremolo...
I know what it needs...
Be right back!
There we go!
Much better!
Bravo!

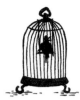

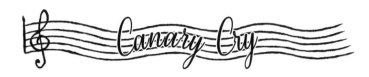

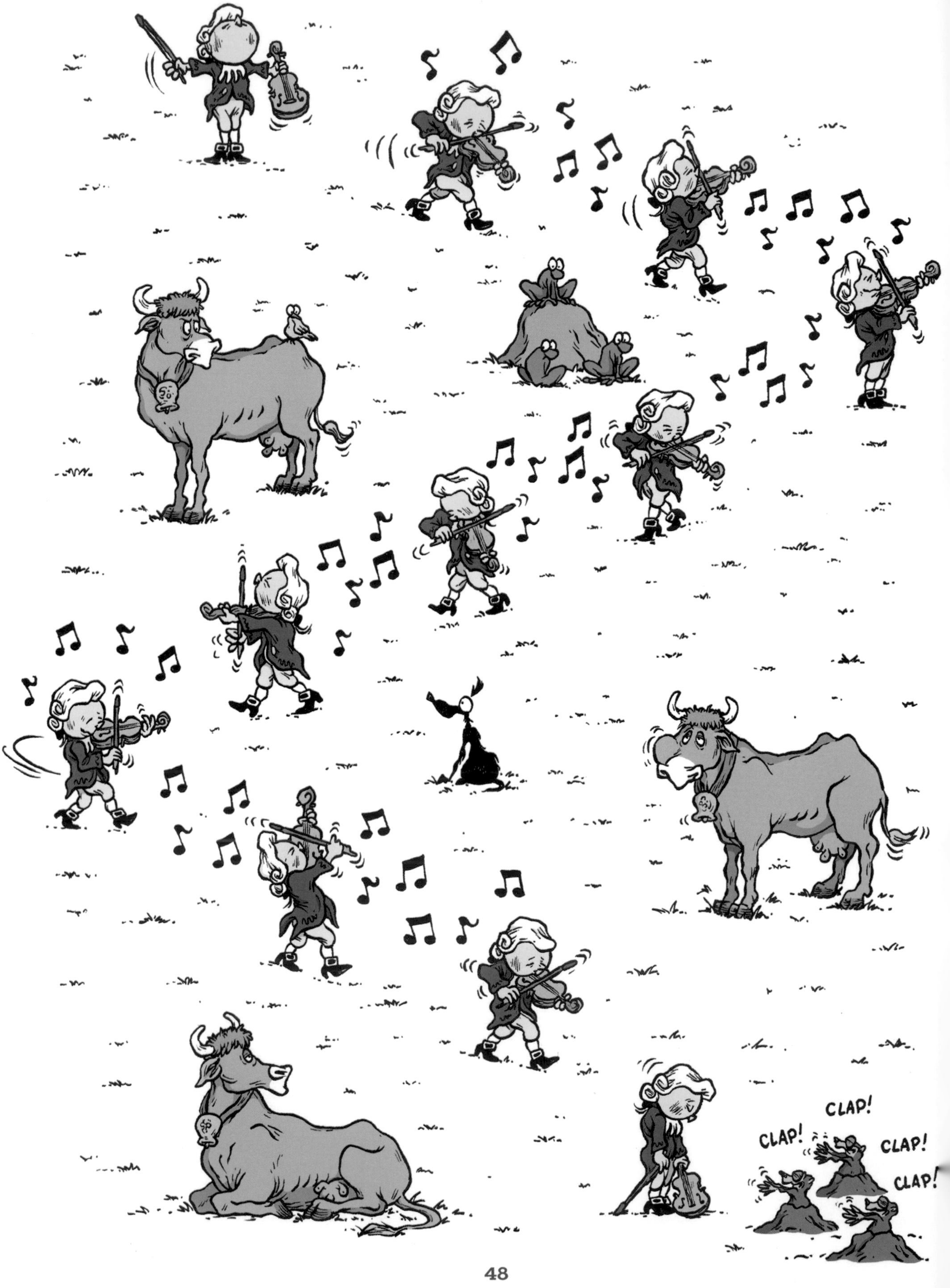
CLAP!
CLAP!
CLAP!
CLAP!

Out of Tune

This is *not* my harpsichord!

It's just out of tune. The tuner should be here any minute!

I'm sorry, I didn't recognize you...

It's like he's lost his voice...

Wolferl, find something else to do!

I can't just abandon him like that! When he needs me most!

Glong Kling

Kloc Dang Gelong

Is it serious, doctor?

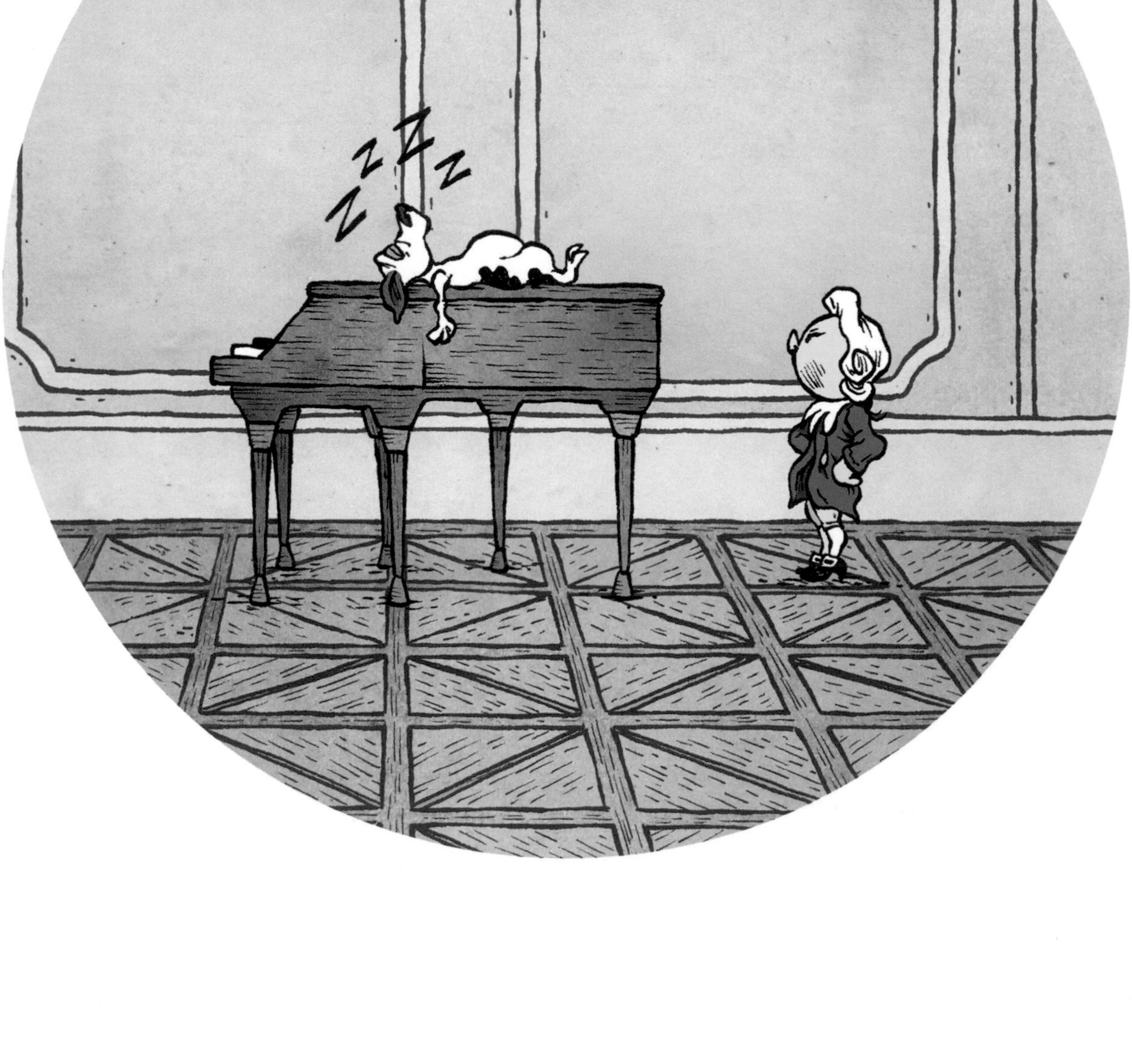
ZZZZZ

Missing!

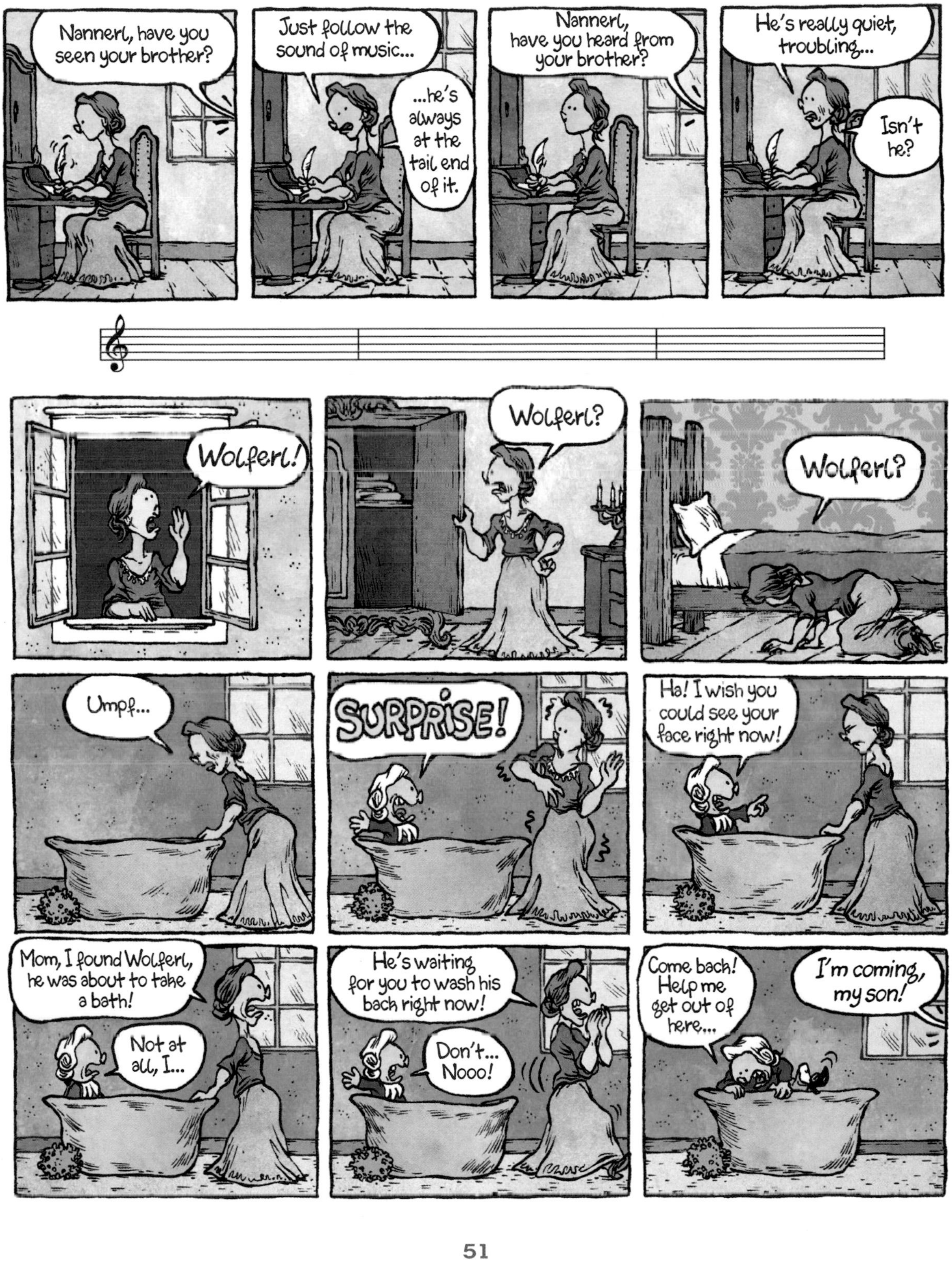

Nannerl, have you seen your brother?
Just follow the sound of music...
...he's always at the tail end of it.
Nannerl, have you heard from your brother?
He's really quiet, troubling...
Isn't he?
Wolferl!
Wolferl?
Wolferl?
Umpf...
SURPRISE!
Ha! I wish you could see your face right now!
Mom, I found Wolferl, he was about to take a bath!
Not at all, I...
He's waiting for you to wash his back right now!
Don't... Nooo!
Come back! Help me get out of here...
I'm coming, my son!

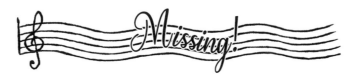

By the Sea

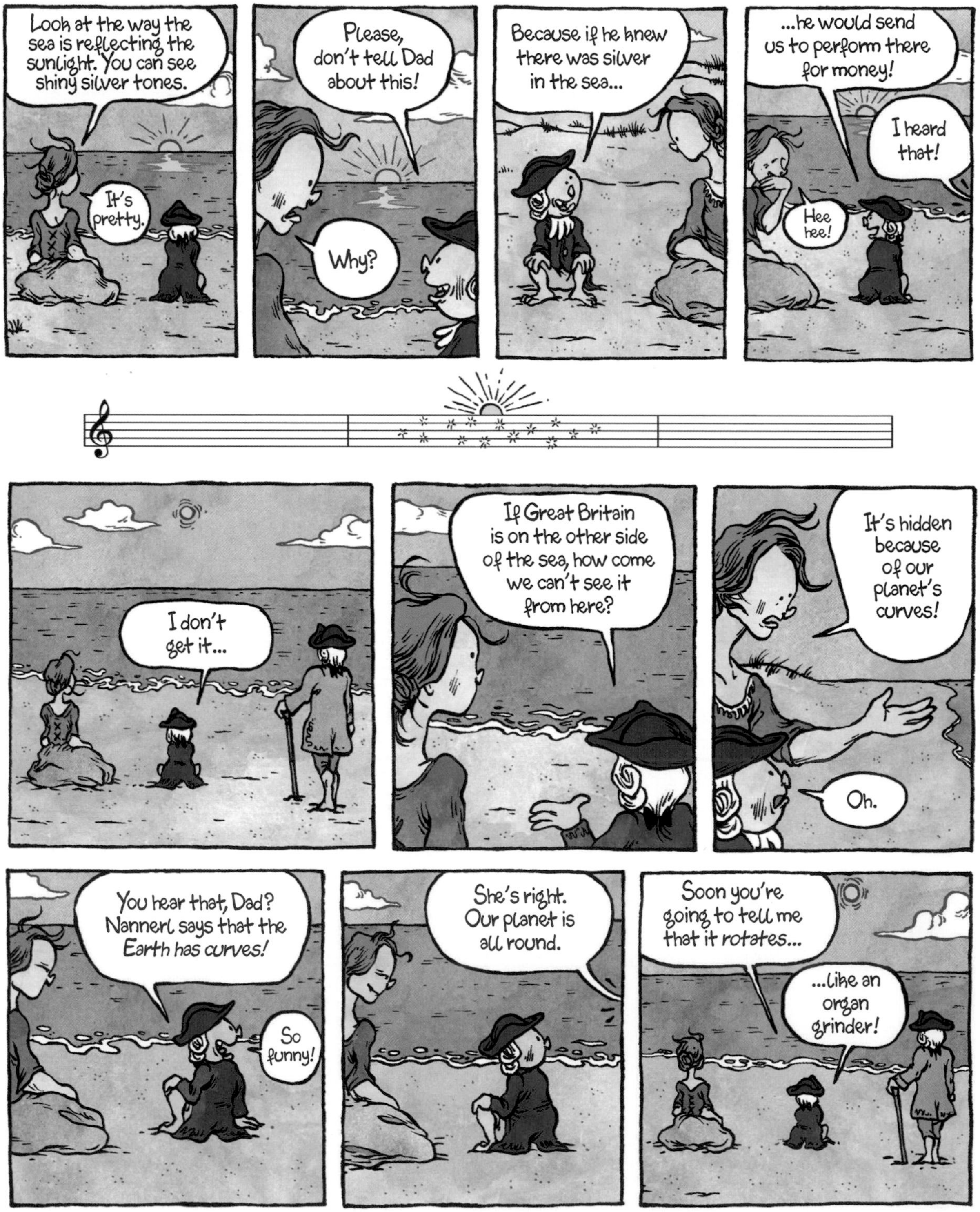
Look at the way the sea is reflecting the sunlight. You can see shiny silver tones.
It's pretty.
Please, don't tell Dad about this!
Why?
Because if he knew there was silver in the sea...
...he would send us to perform there for money!
Hee hee!
I heard that!
I don't get it...
If Great Britain is on the other side of the sea, how come we can't see it from here?
It's hidden because of our planet's curves!
Oh.
You hear that, Dad? Nannerl says that the Earth has curves!
So funny!
She's right. Our planet is all round.
Soon you're going to tell me that it rotates...
...like an organ grinder!

  **Picture Perfect**

 Are we done yet?

 Far from it... I'm still sketching...

 Sketching?
But...
...You don't paint directly?

 You think I sketch when I write music?
Your pose, sir. Please.

 Herr Mozart, I'm begging you...

 ...could you sit still while I'm drawing your portrait?

 Right. Then, you shouldn't have put that harpsichord here.

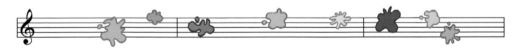

 Is this a painting of Pimberl sleeping?
Yes.

 Wasn't this artist supposed to draw your portrait?
Indeed. But he also said I was insufferable. Pff...

 So he painted Pimberl instead.
Can you believe that?

 It's quite relaxing...
He said that, too.

On the Bench

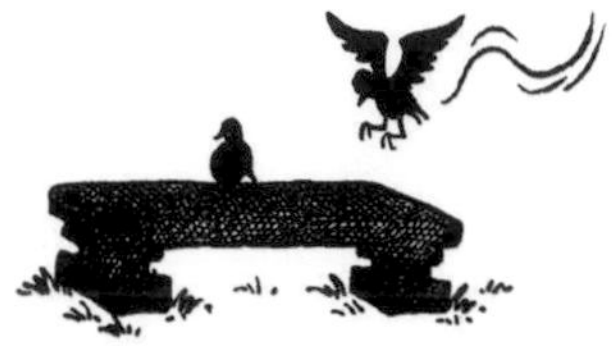

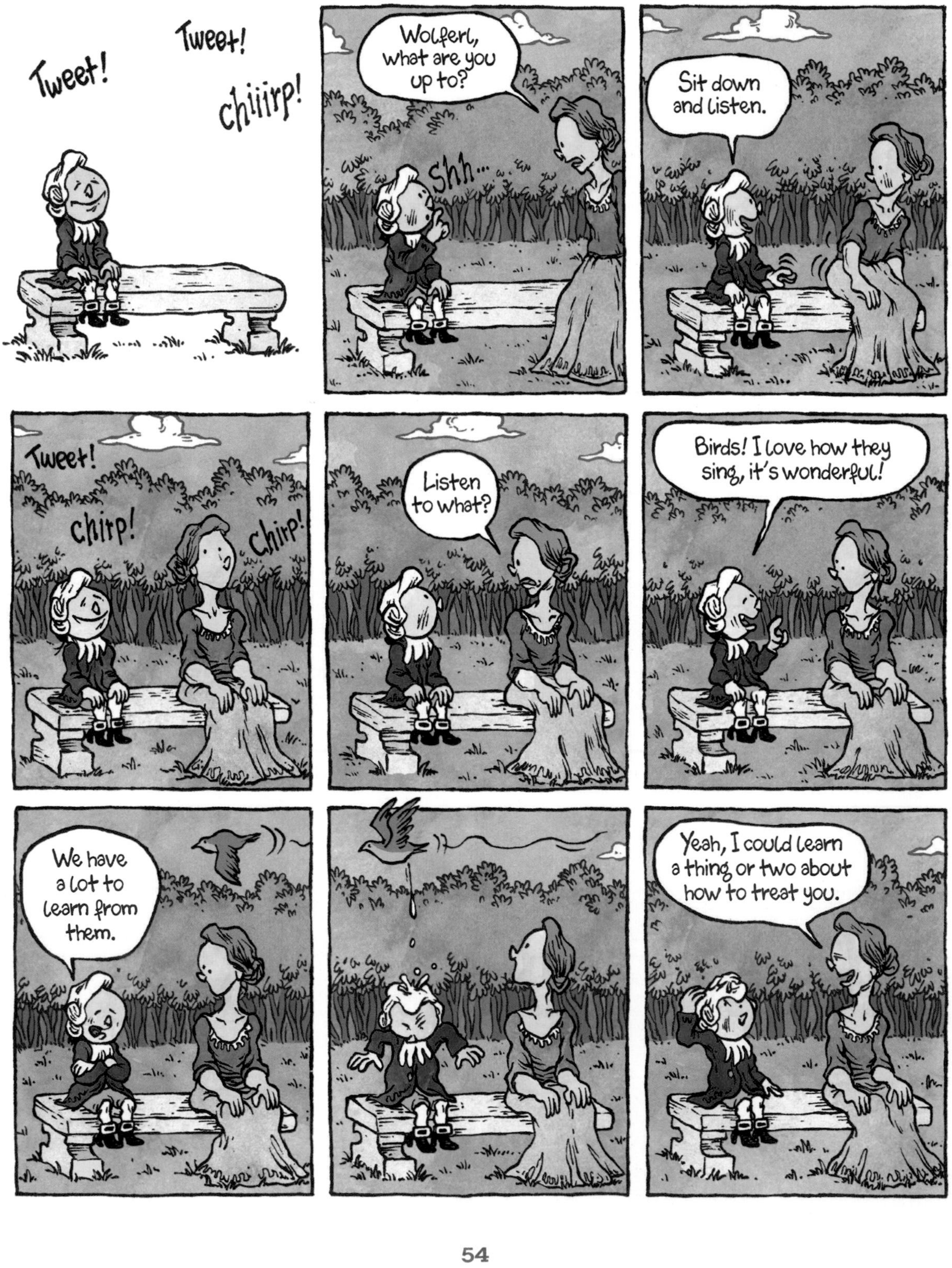

Tweet!
Tweet!
chiiirp!
Wolferl, what are you up to?
Shh...
Sit down and listen.
Tweet!
chirp!
Chirp!
Listen to what?
Birds! I love how they sing, it's wonderful!
We have a lot to learn from them.
Yeah, I could learn a thing or two about how to treat you.

The Notebook

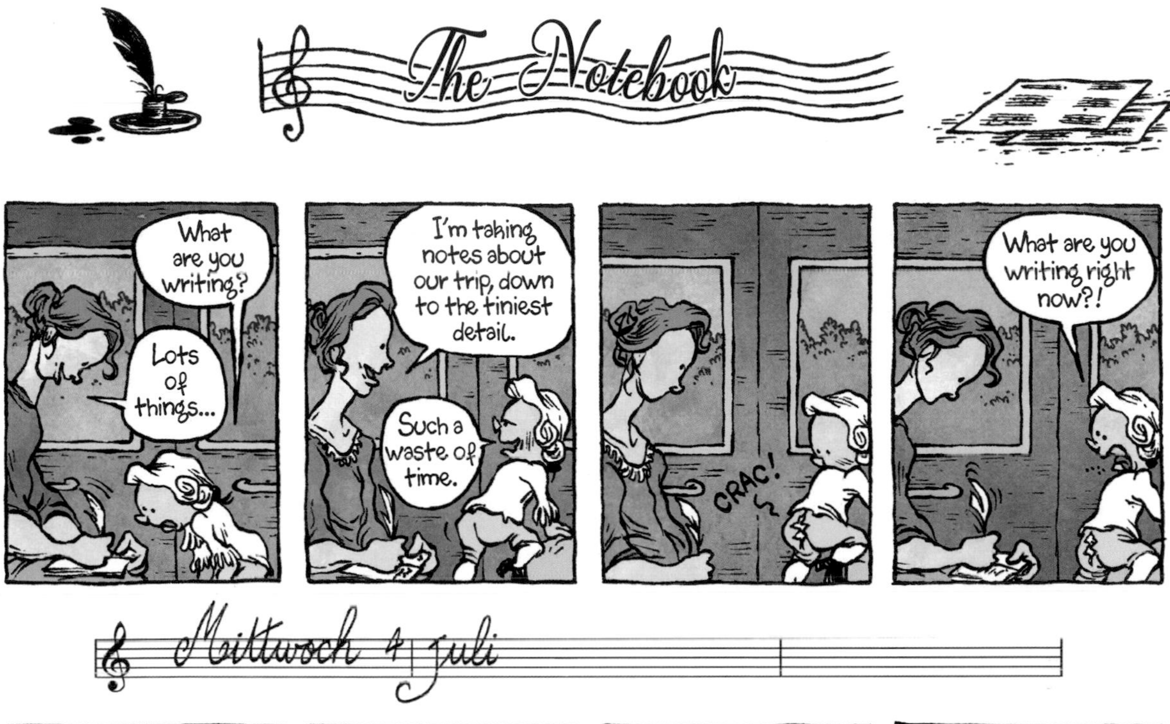

What are you writing?
Lots of things...
I'm taking notes about our trip, down to the tiniest detail.
Such a waste of time.
CRAC!
What are you writing right now?!

Mittwoch 4 Juli

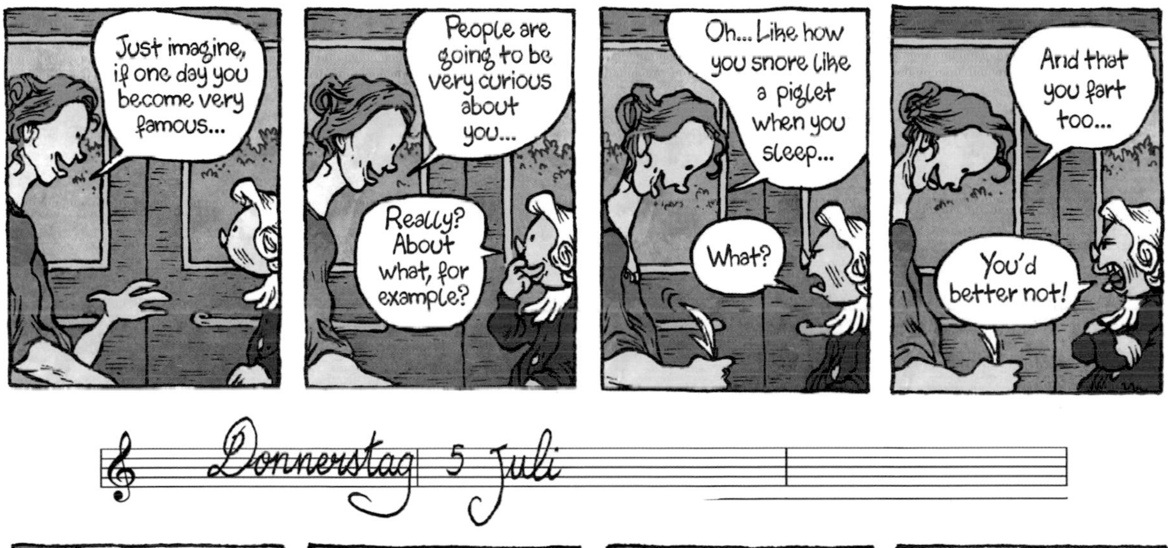

Just imagine, if one day you become very famous...
People are going to be very curious about you...
Really? About what, for example?
Oh... Like how you snore like a piglet when you sleep...
What?
And that you fart too...
You'd better not!

Donnerstag 5 Juli

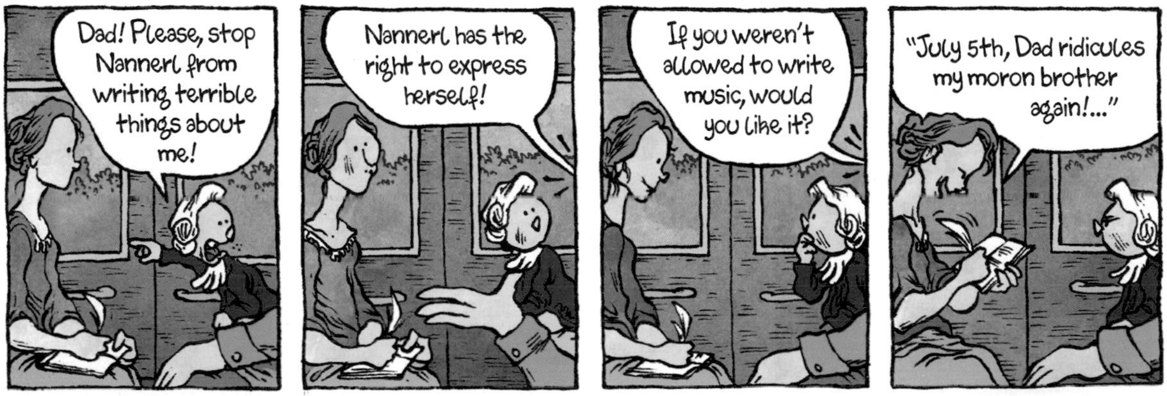

Dad! Please, stop Nannerl from writing terrible things about me!
Nannerl has the right to express herself!
If you weren't allowed to write music, would you like it?
"July 5th, Dad ridicules my moron brother again!..."

The Spider

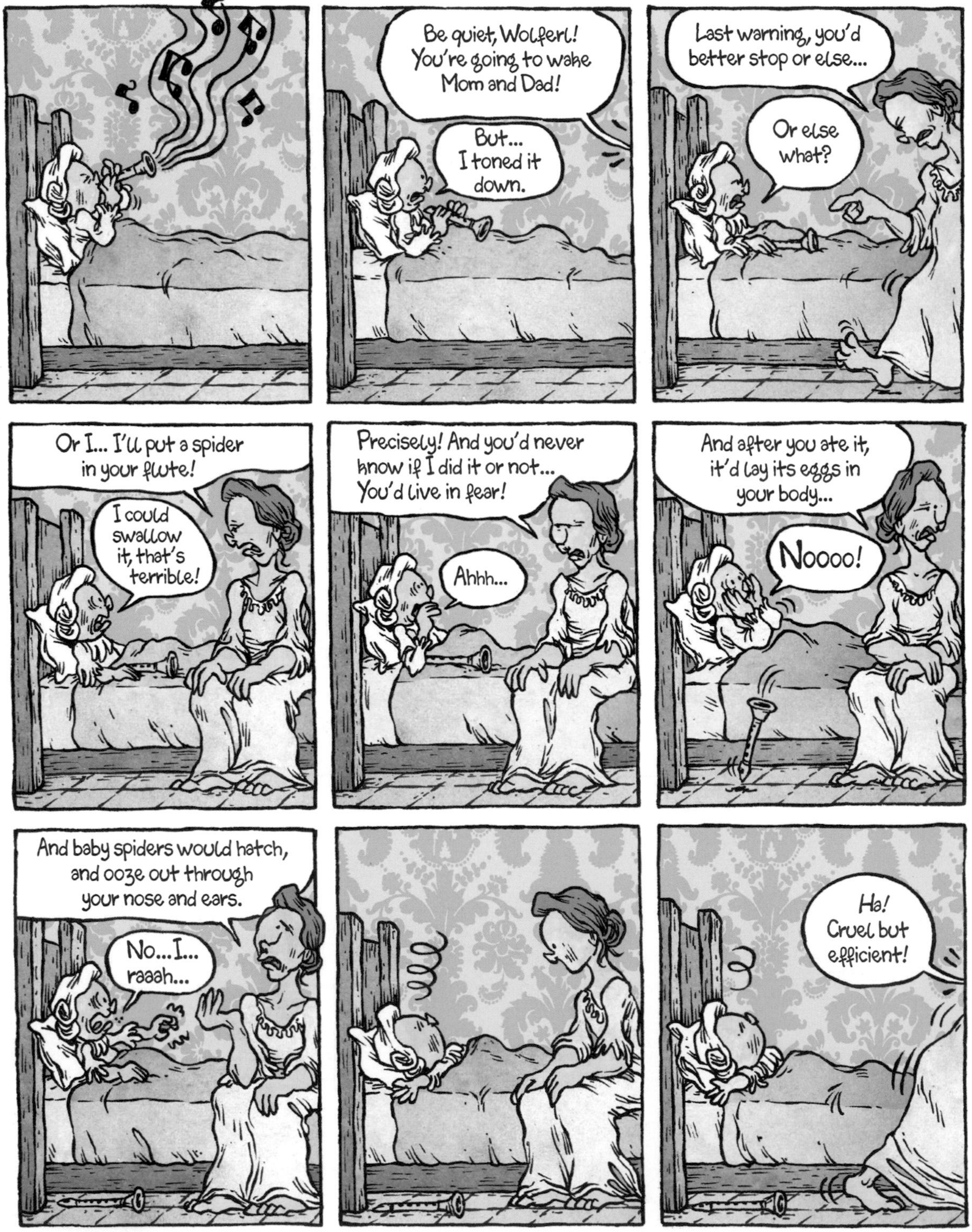
Be quiet, Wolferl! You're going to wake Mom and Dad!
But... I toned it down.
Last warning, you'd better stop or else...
Or else what?
Or I... I'll put a spider in your flute!
I could swallow it, that's terrible!
Precisely! And you'd never know if I did it or not... You'd live in fear!
Ahhh...
And after you ate it, it'd lay its eggs in your body...
Noooo!
And baby spiders would hatch, and ooze out through your nose and ears.
No... I... raaah...
Ha! Cruel but efficient!

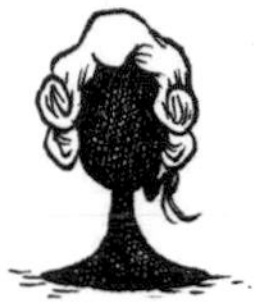

Gone With the Wig

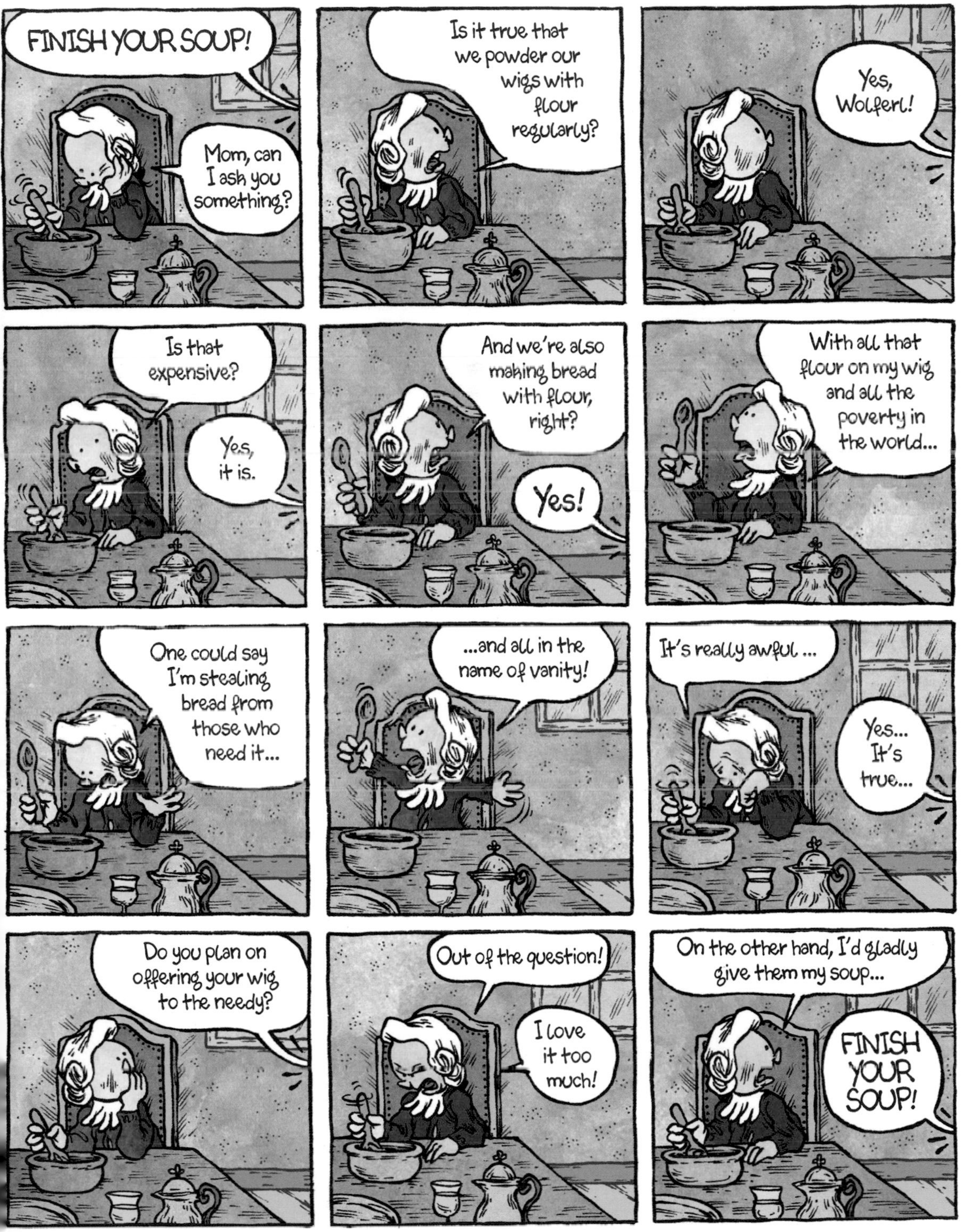
FINISH YOUR SOUP!
Mom, can I ask you something?
Is it true that we powder our wigs with flour regularly?
Yes, Wolferl!
Is that expensive?
Yes, it is.
And we're also making bread with flour, right?
Yes!
With all that flour on my wig and all the poverty in the world...
One could say I'm stealing bread from those who need it...
...and all in the name of vanity!
It's really awful ...
Yes... It's true...
Do you plan on offering your wig to the needy?
Out of the question!
I love it too much!
On the other hand, I'd gladly give them my soup...
FINISH YOUR SOUP!

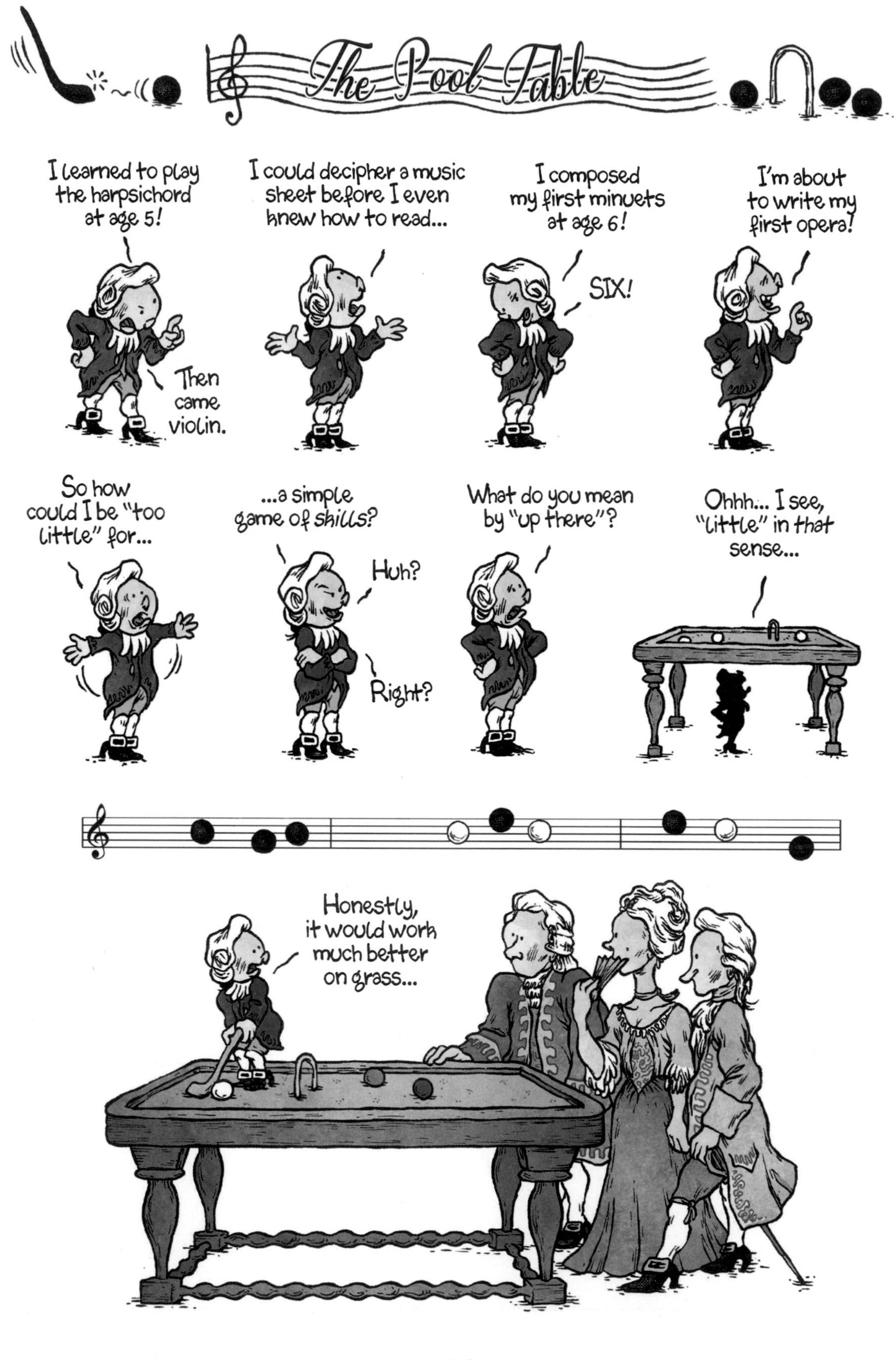
The Pool Table
I learned to play the harpsichord at age 5!
Then came violin.
I could decipher a music sheet before I even knew how to read...
I composed my first minuets at age 6!
SIX!
I'm about to write my first opera!
So how could I be "too little" for...
...a simple game of skills?
Huh?
Right?
What do you mean by "up there"?
Ohhh... I see, "little" in that sense...
Honestly, it would work much better on grass...

The Soup

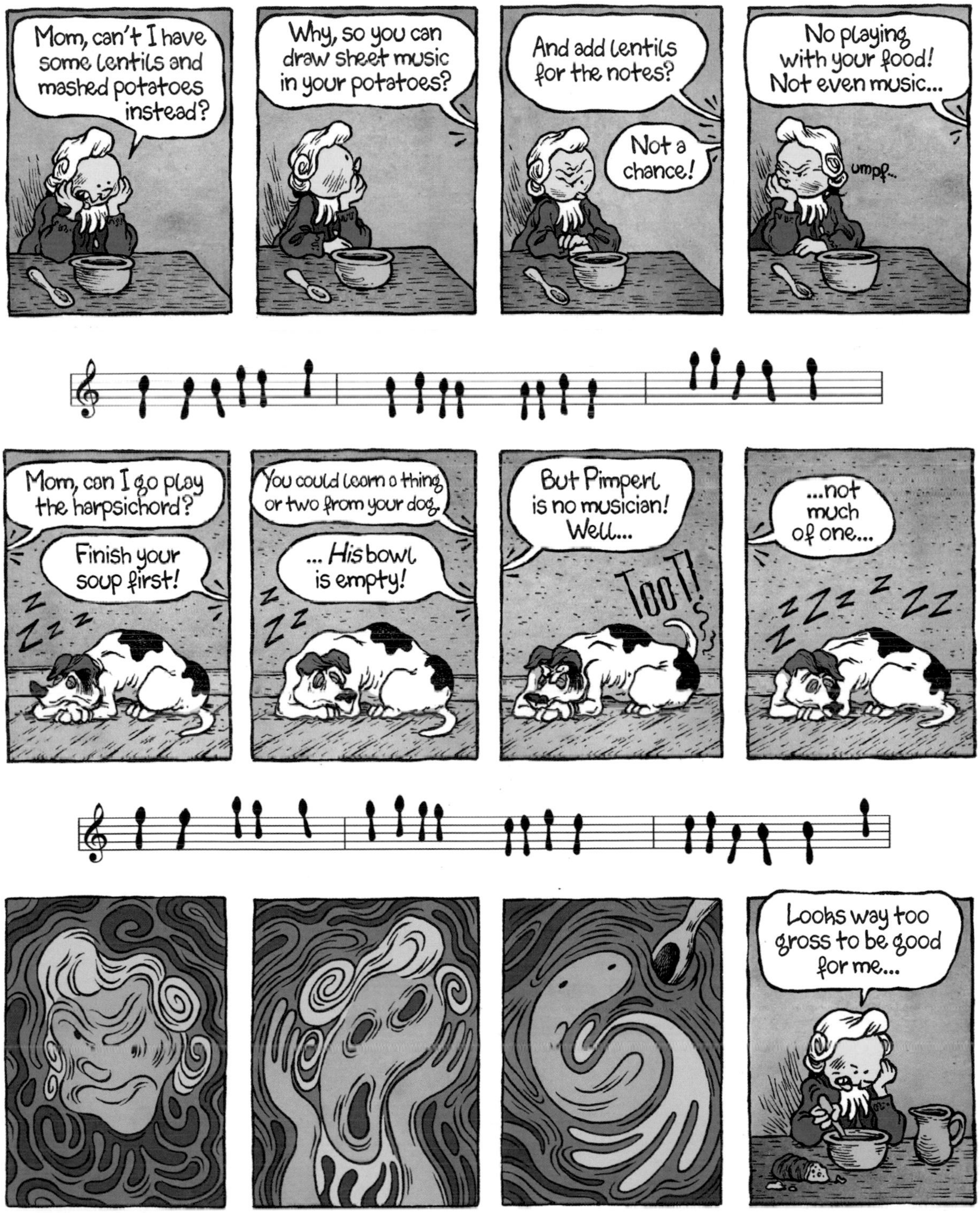

Mom, can't I have some lentils and mashed potatoes instead?
Why, so you can draw sheet music in your potatoes?
And add lentils for the notes?
Not a chance!
No playing with your food! Not even music...
umpf...
Mom, can I go play the harpsichord?
Finish your soup first!
You could learn a thing or two from your dog.
... His bowl is empty!
But Pimperl is no musician! Well...
TOOT!
...not much of one...
Looks way too gross to be good for me...

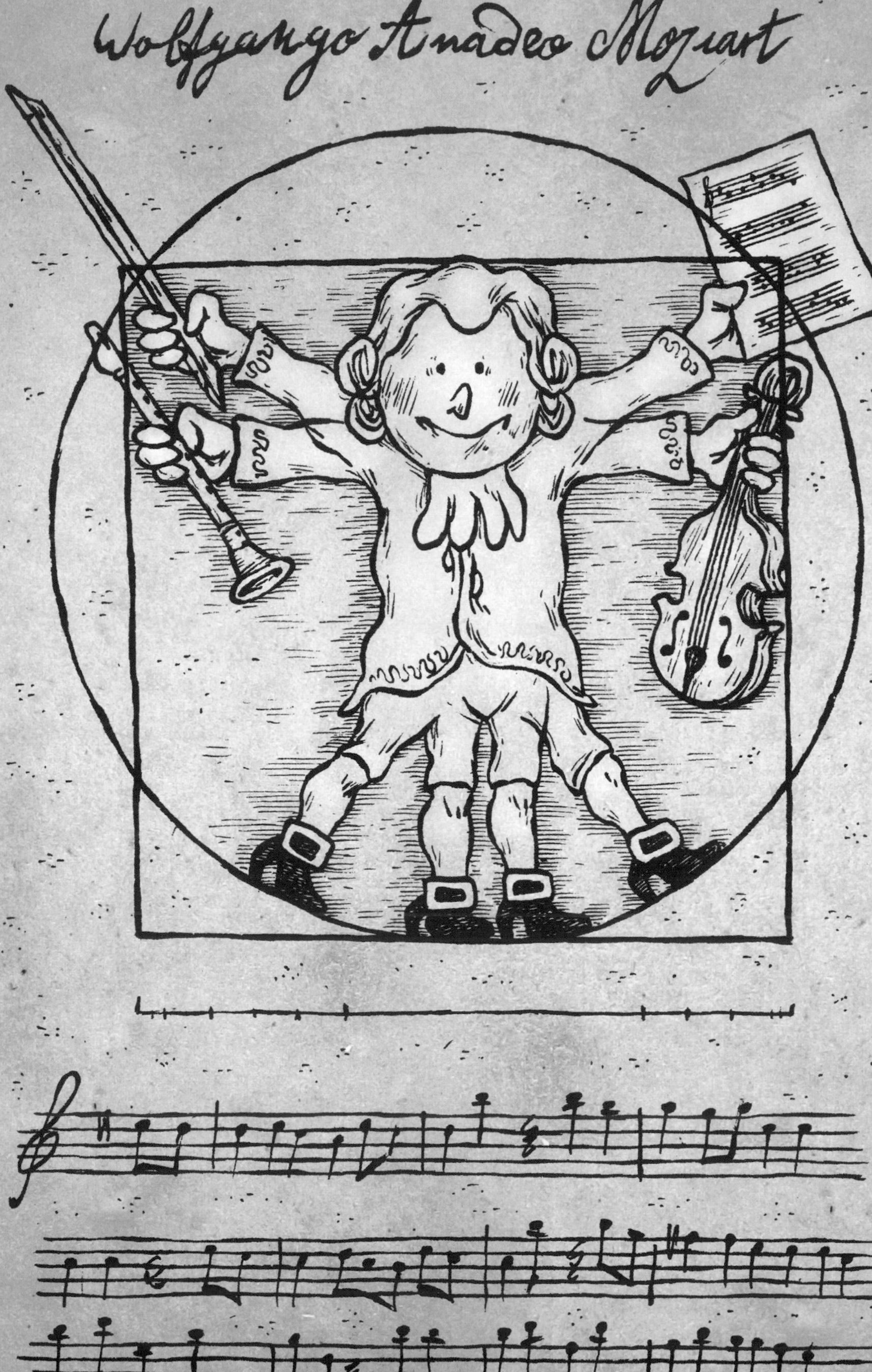
Wolfgango Amadeo Mozart

The Toothpick Box

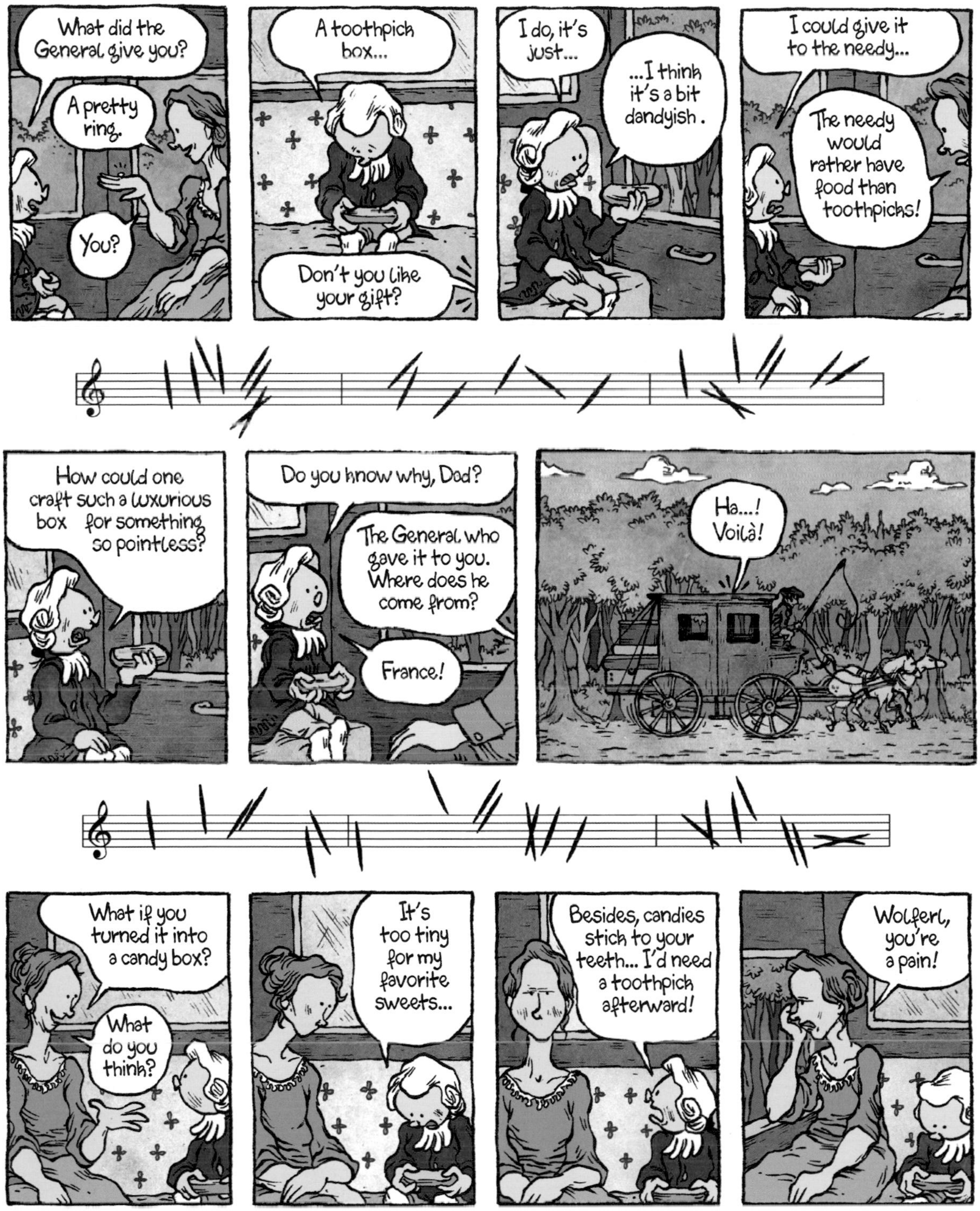
What did the General give you?
A pretty ring.
You?
A toothpick box...
Don't you like your gift?
I do, it's just...
...I think it's a bit dandyish.
I could give it to the needy...
The needy would rather have food than toothpicks!
How could one craft such a luxurious box for something so pointless?
Do you know why, Dad?
The General who gave it to you. Where does he come from?
France!
Ha...! Voilà!
What if you turned it into a candy box?
What do you think?
It's too tiny for my favorite sweets...
Besides, candies stick to your teeth... I'd need a toothpick afterward!
Wolferl, you're a pain!

Quill Issues

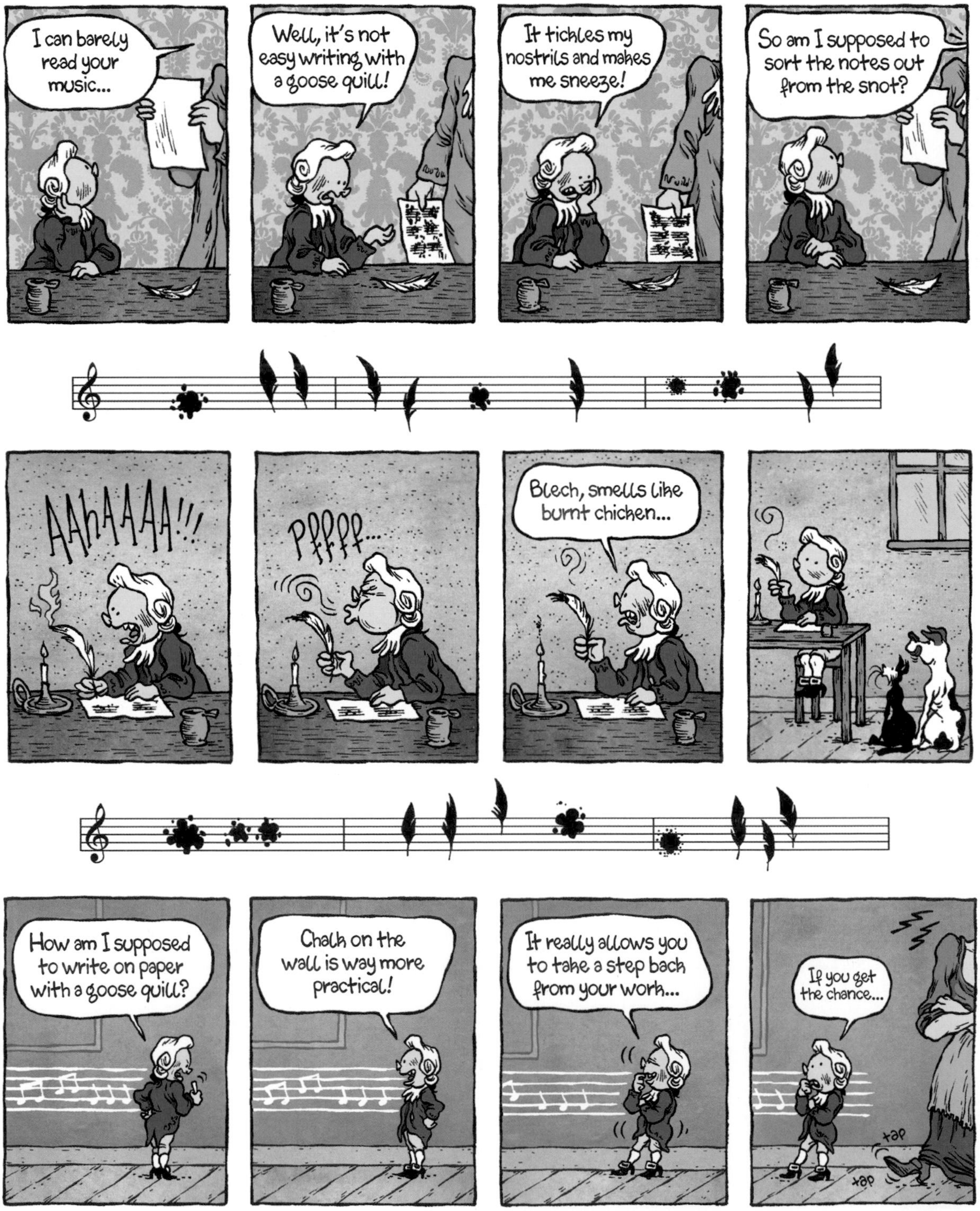
I can barely read your music...
Well, it's not easy writing with a goose quill!
It tickles my nostrils and makes me sneeze!
So am I supposed to sort the notes out from the snot?
AAhAAAA!!!
Pffff...
Blech, smells like burnt chicken...
How am I supposed to write on paper with a goose quill?
Chalk on the wall is way more practical!
It really allows you to take a step back from your work...
If you get the chance...
tap
tap

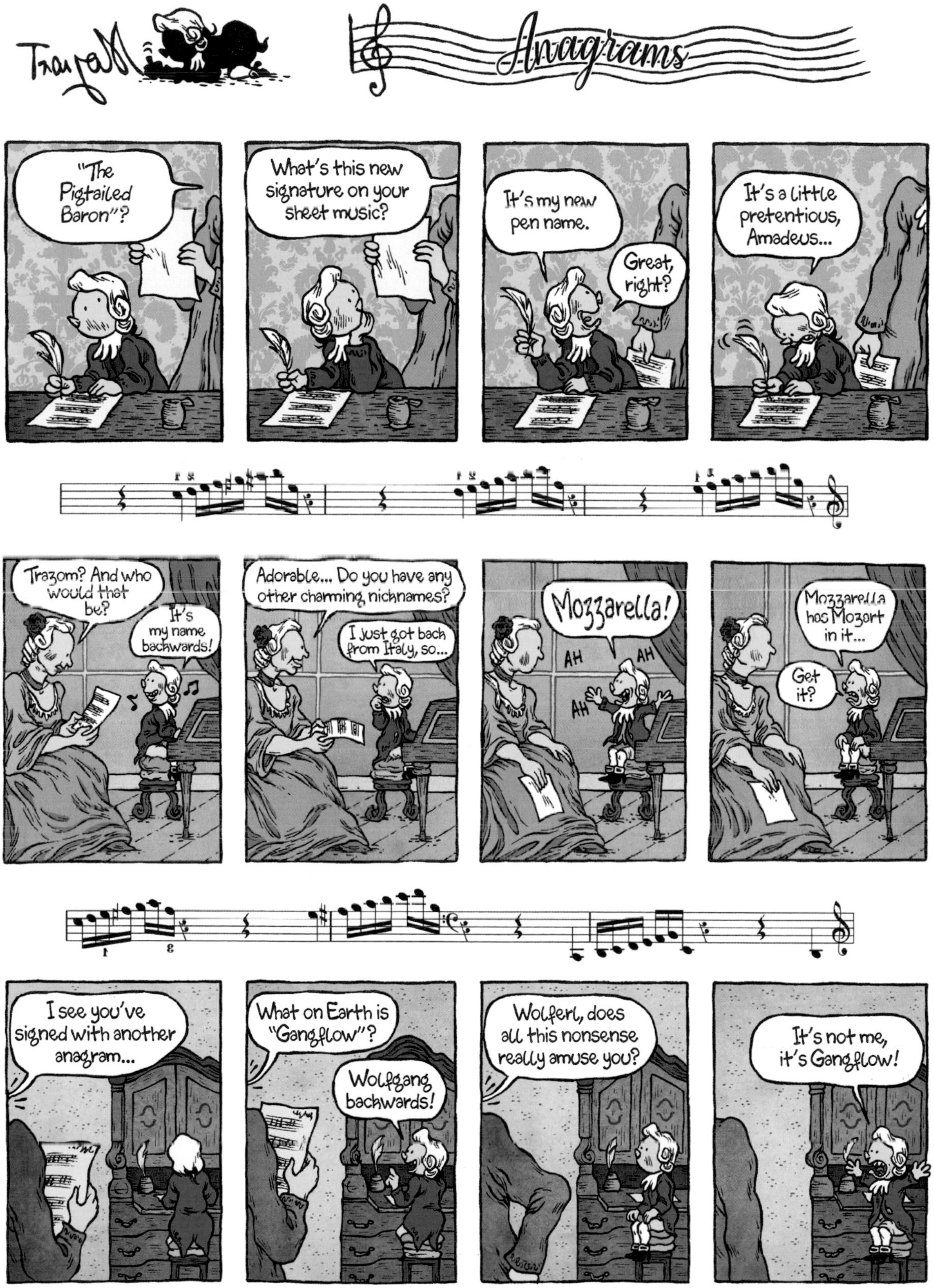
Trazom
Anagrams
"The Pigtailed Baron"?
What's this new signature on your sheet music?
It's my new pen name.
Great, right?
It's a little pretentious, Amadeus...
Trazom? And who would that be?
It's my name backwards!
Adorable... Do you have any other charming nicknames?
I just got back from Italy, so...
Mozzarella!
AH AH AH
Mozzarella has Mozart in it...
Get it?
I see you've signed with another anagram...
What on Earth is "Gangflow"?
Wolfgang backwards!
Wolferl, does all this nonsense really amuse you?
It's not me, it's Gangflow!

Your Highness

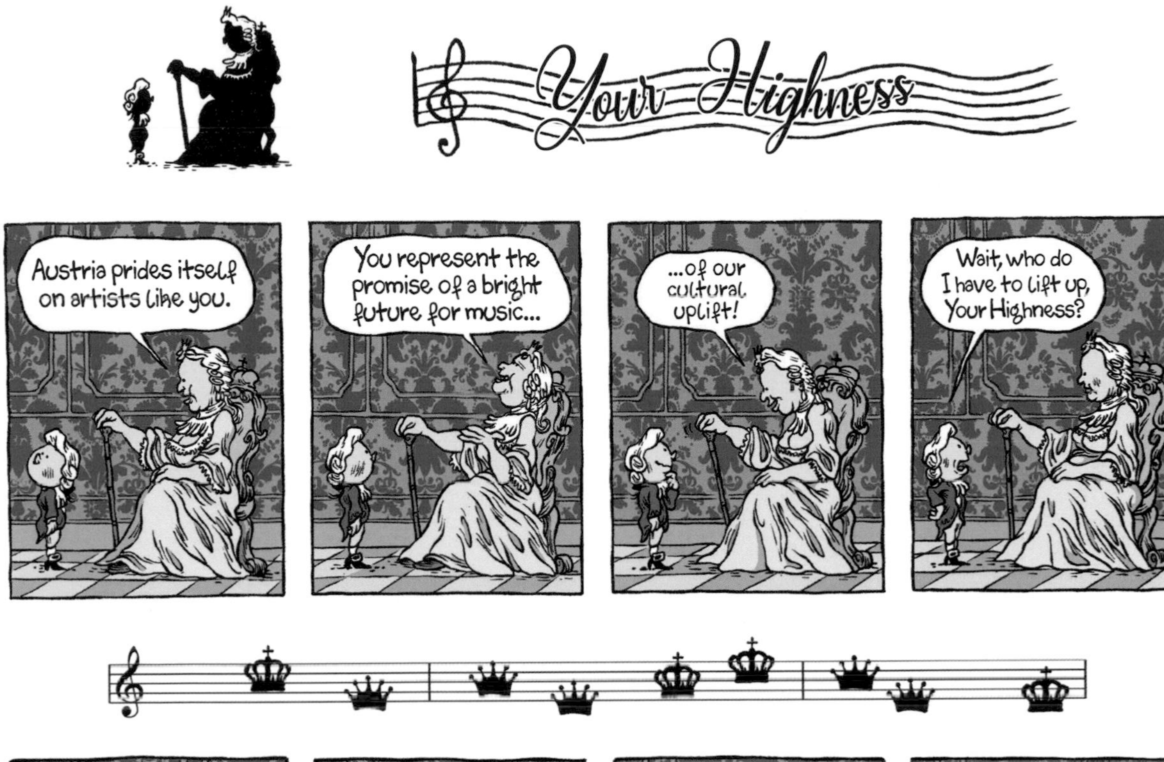
Austria prides itself on artists like you.
You represent the promise of a bright future for music...
...of our cultural uplift!
Wait, who do I have to lift up, Your Highness?

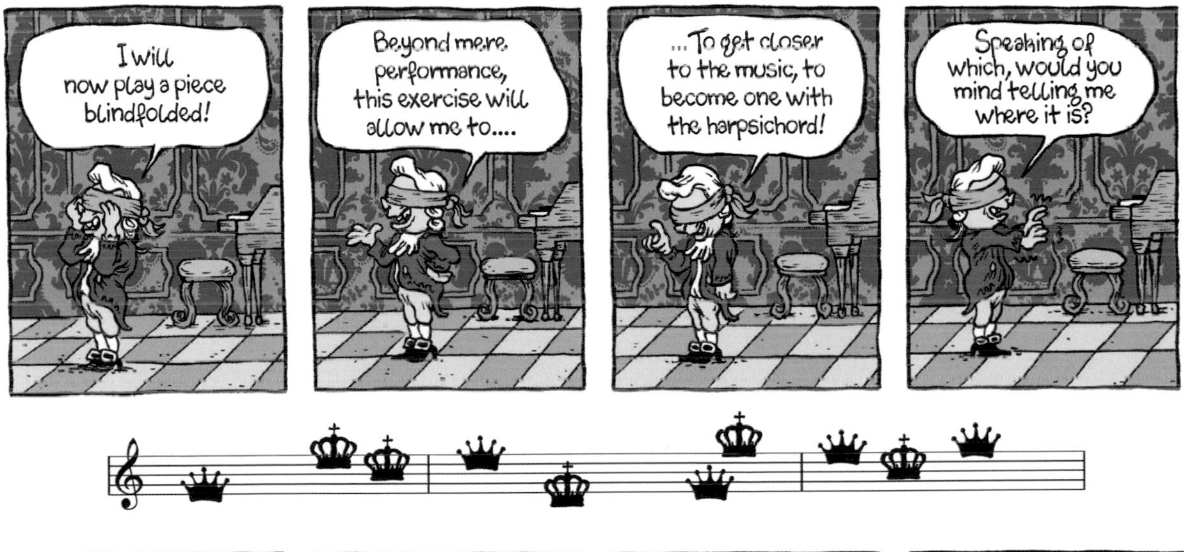
I will now play a piece blindfolded!
Beyond mere performance, this exercise will allow me to....
...To get closer to the music, to become one with the harpsichord!
Speaking of which, would you mind telling me where it is?

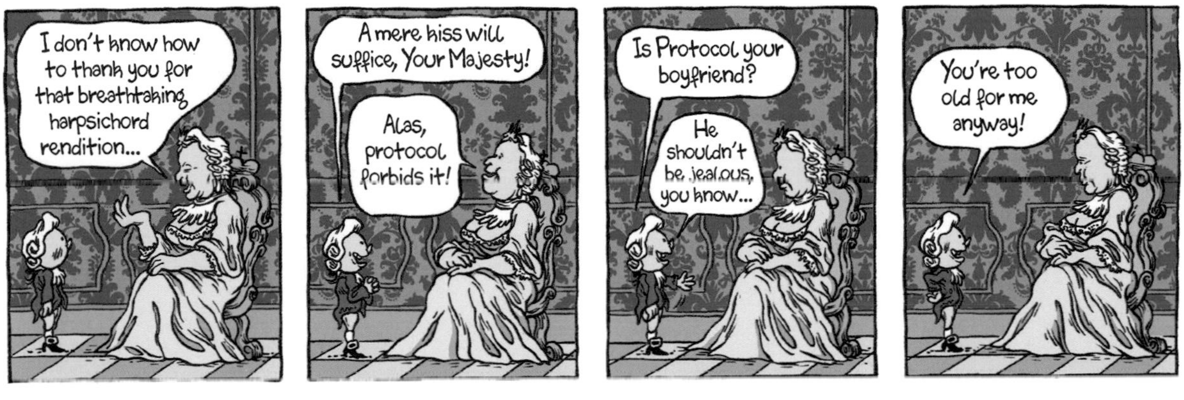
I don't know how to thank you for that breathtaking harpsichord rendition...
A mere kiss will suffice, Your Majesty!
Alas, protocol forbids it!
Is Protocol your boyfriend?
He shouldn't be jealous, you know...
You're too old for me anyway!

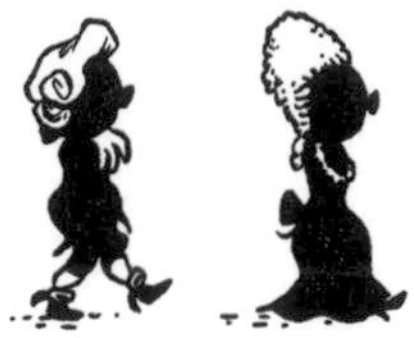

Girls!

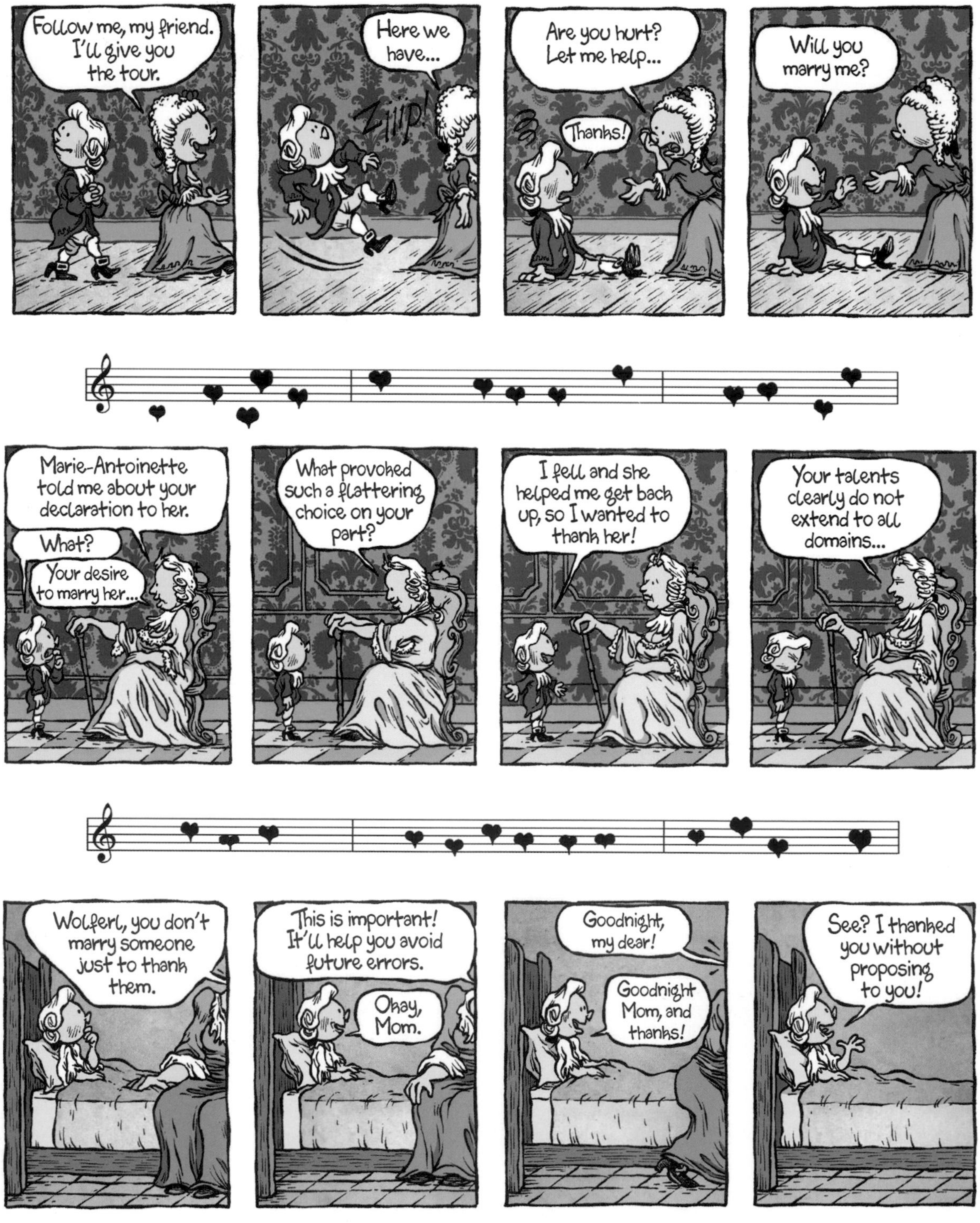
Follow me, my friend. I'll give you the tour.
Here we have...
Zziip!
Are you hurt? Let me help...
Thanks!
Will you marry me?
Marie-Antoinette told me about your declaration to her.
What?
Your desire to marry her...
What provoked such a flattering choice on your part?
I fell and she helped me get back up, so I wanted to thank her!
Your talents clearly do not extend to all domains...
Wolferl, you don't marry someone just to thank them.
This is important! It'll help you avoid future errors.
Okay, Mom.
Goodnight, my dear!
Goodnight Mom, and thanks!
See? I thanked you without proposing to you!

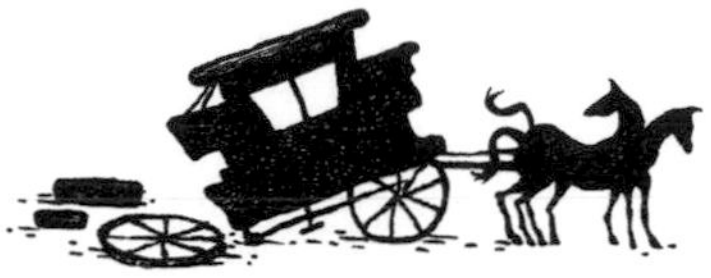

Off the Beaten Path

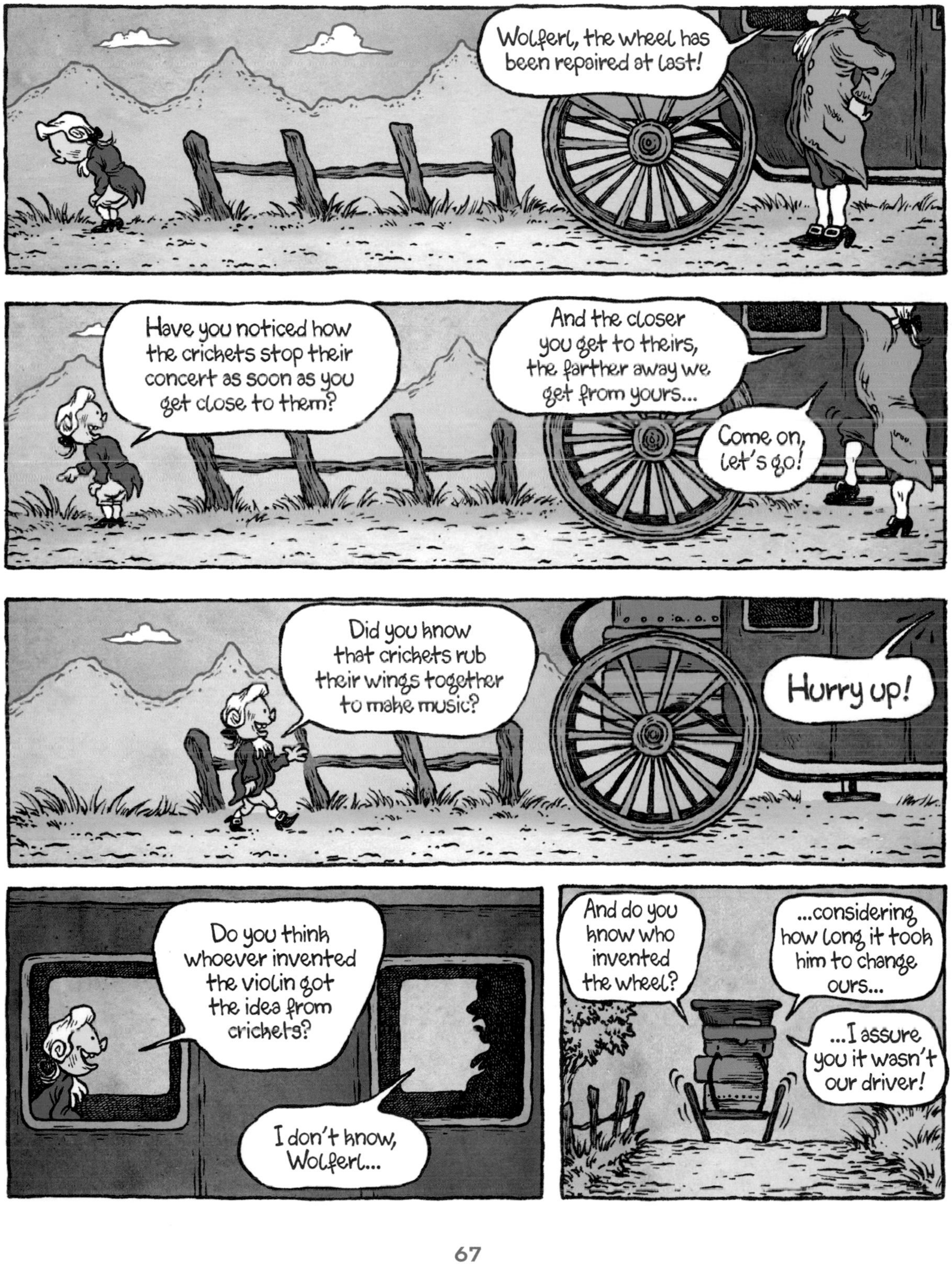
Wolferl, the wheel has been repaired at last!
Have you noticed how the crickets stop their concert as soon as you get close to them?
And the closer you get to theirs, the farther away we get from yours...
Come on, let's go!
Did you know that crickets rub their wings together to make music?
Hurry up!
Do you think whoever invented the violin got the idea from crickets?
I don't know, Wolferl...
And do you know who invented the wheel?
...considering how long it took him to change ours...
...I assure you it wasn't our driver!

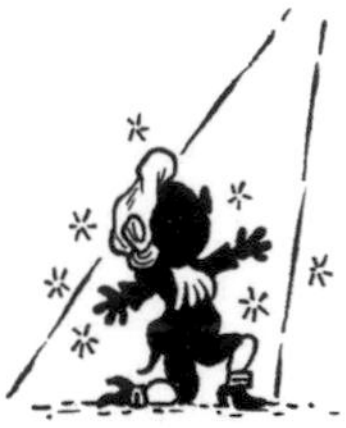

Deo Gratias

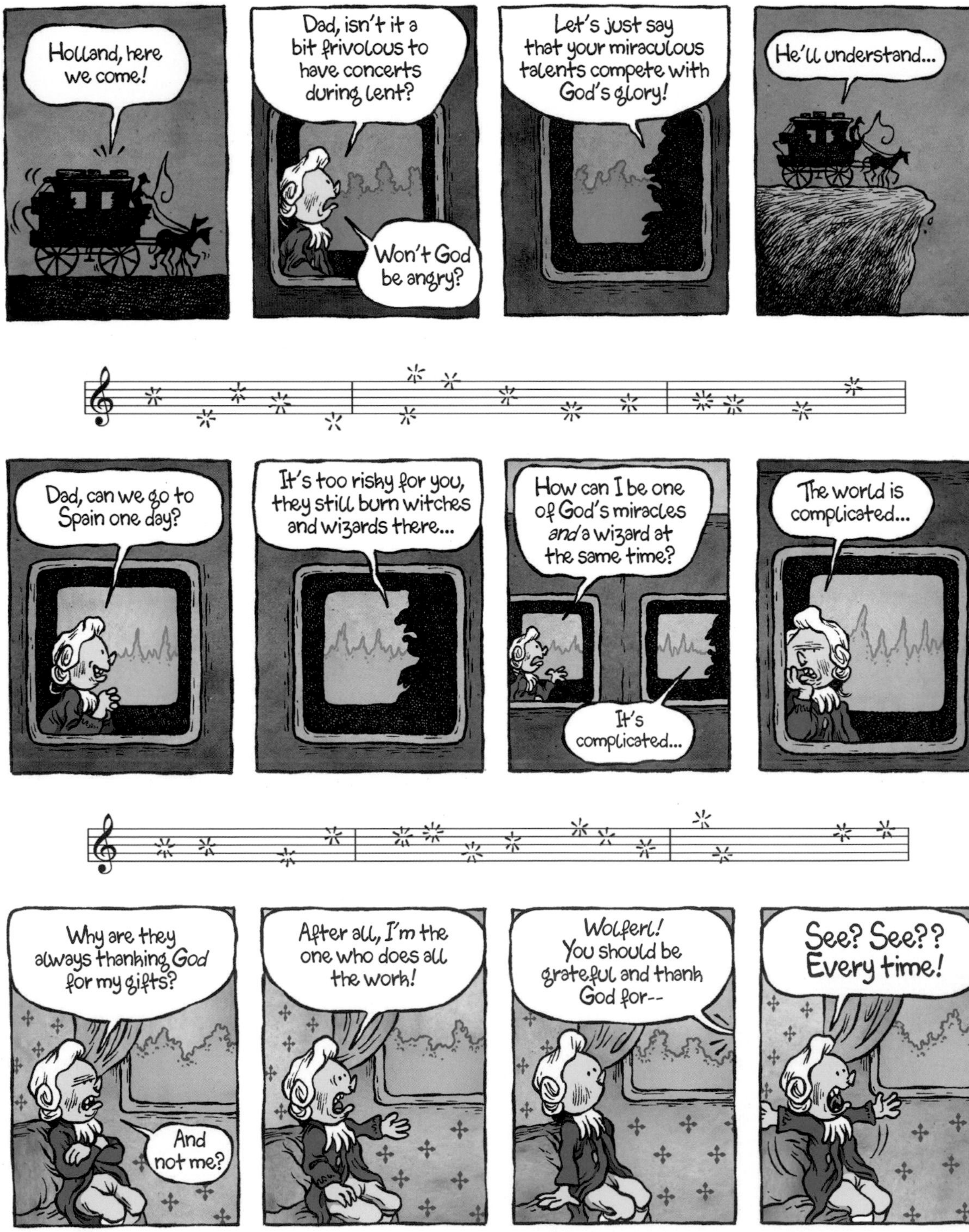

Holland, here we come!
Dad, isn't it a bit frivolous to have concerts during lent?
Won't God be angry?
Let's just say that your miraculous talents compete with God's glory!
He'll understand...
Dad, can we go to Spain one day?
It's too risky for you, they still burn witches and wizards there...
How can I be one of God's miracles *and* a wizard at the same time?
It's complicated...
The world is complicated...
Why are they always thanking *God* for my gifts?
And not me?
After all, I'm the one who does all the work!
Wolferl! You should be grateful and thank God for--
See? See?? Every time!

Pirates!

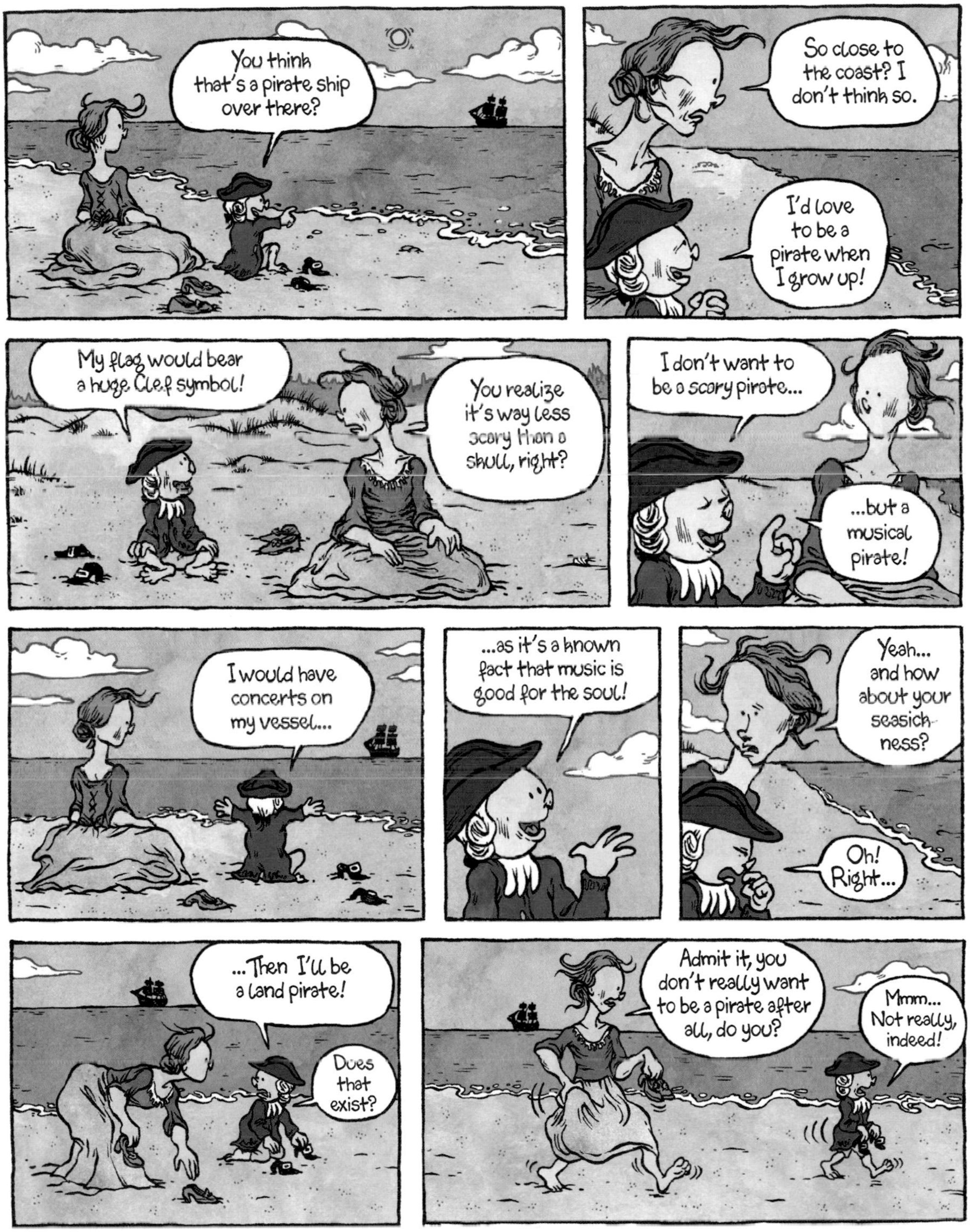
You think that's a pirate ship over there?
So close to the coast? I don't think so.
I'd love to be a pirate when I grow up!
My flag would bear a huge Clef symbol!
You realize it's way less scary than a skull, right?
I don't want to be a scary pirate...
...but a musical pirate!
I would have concerts on my vessel...
...as it's a known fact that music is good for the soul!
Yeah... and how about your seasick-ness?
Oh! Right...
...Then I'll be a land pirate!
Does that exist?
Admit it, you don't really want to be a pirate after all, do you?
Mmm... Not really, indeed!

The Scarf

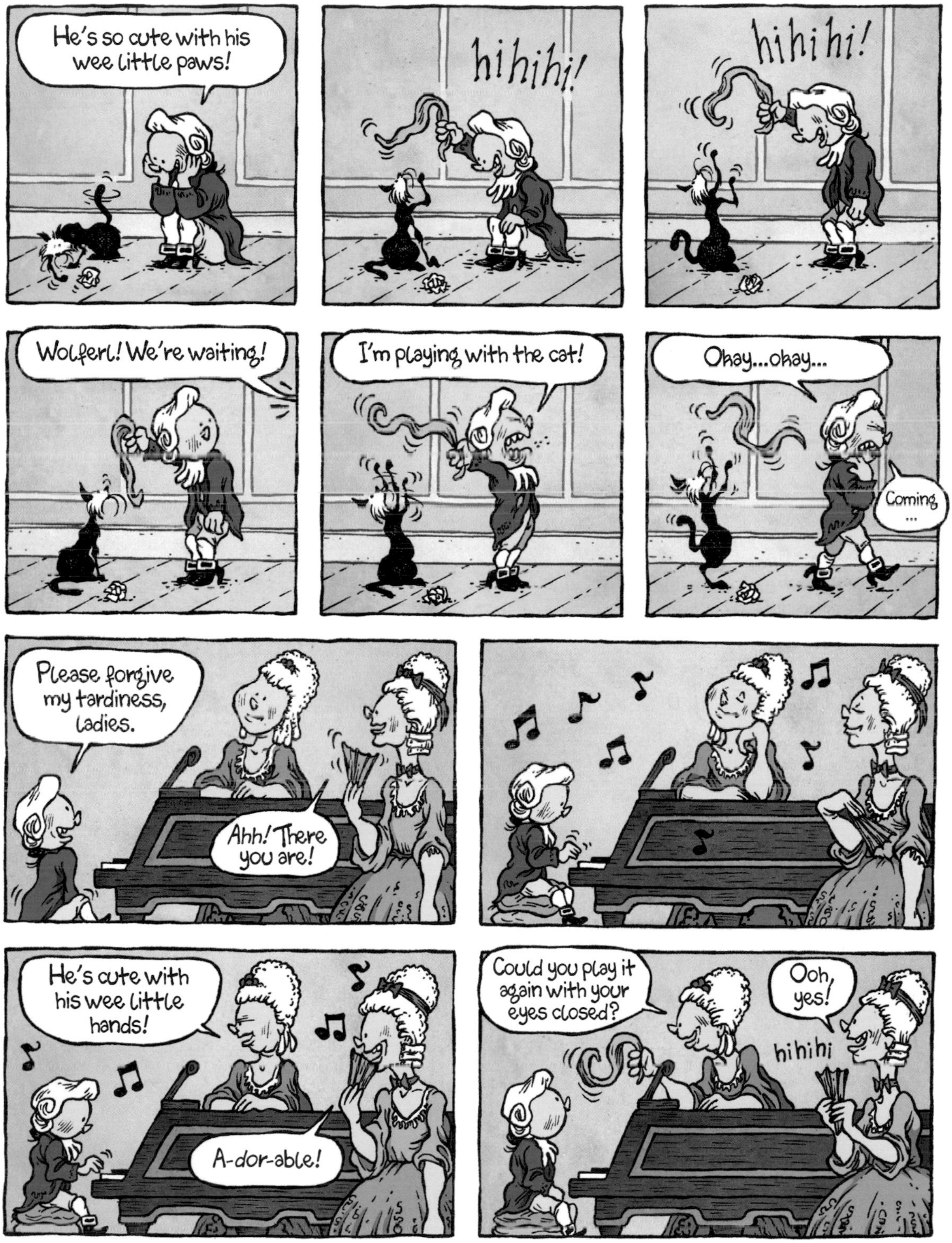
He's so cute with his wee little paws!
hihihi!
hihihi!
Wolferl! We're waiting!
I'm playing with the cat!
Okay...okay...
Coming...
Please forgive my tardiness, ladies.
Ahh! There you are!
He's cute with his wee little hands!
A-dor-able!
Could you play it again with your eyes closed?
Ooh, yes!
hihihi

Up High!

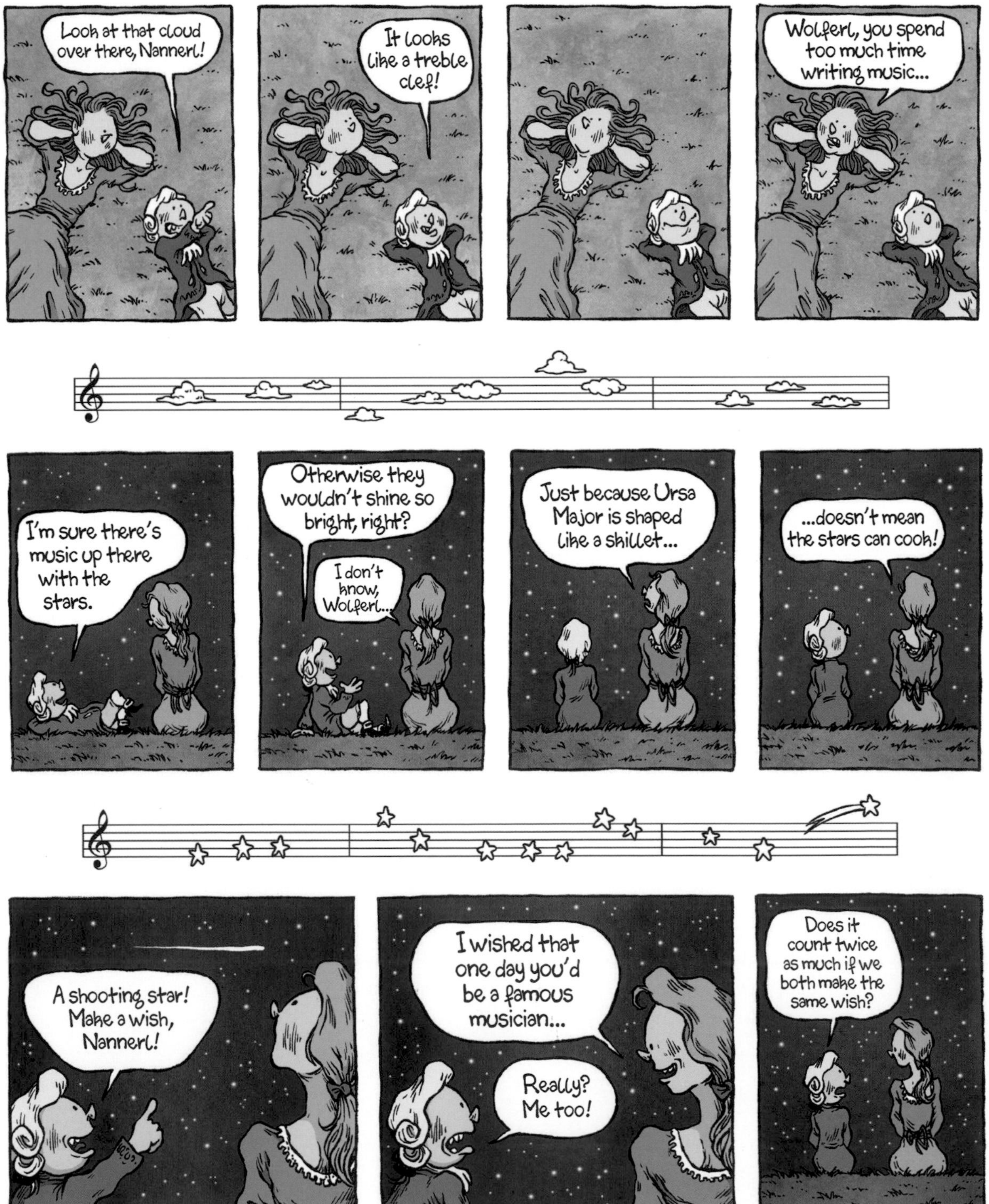
Look at that cloud over there, Nannerl!
It looks like a treble clef!
Wolferl, you spend too much time writing music...
I'm sure there's music up there with the stars.
Otherwise they wouldn't shine so bright, right?
I don't know, Wolferl...
Just because Ursa Major is shaped like a skillet...
...doesn't mean the stars can cook!
A shooting star! Make a wish, Nannerl!
I wished that one day you'd be a famous musician...
Really? Me too!
Does it count twice as much if we both make the same wish?

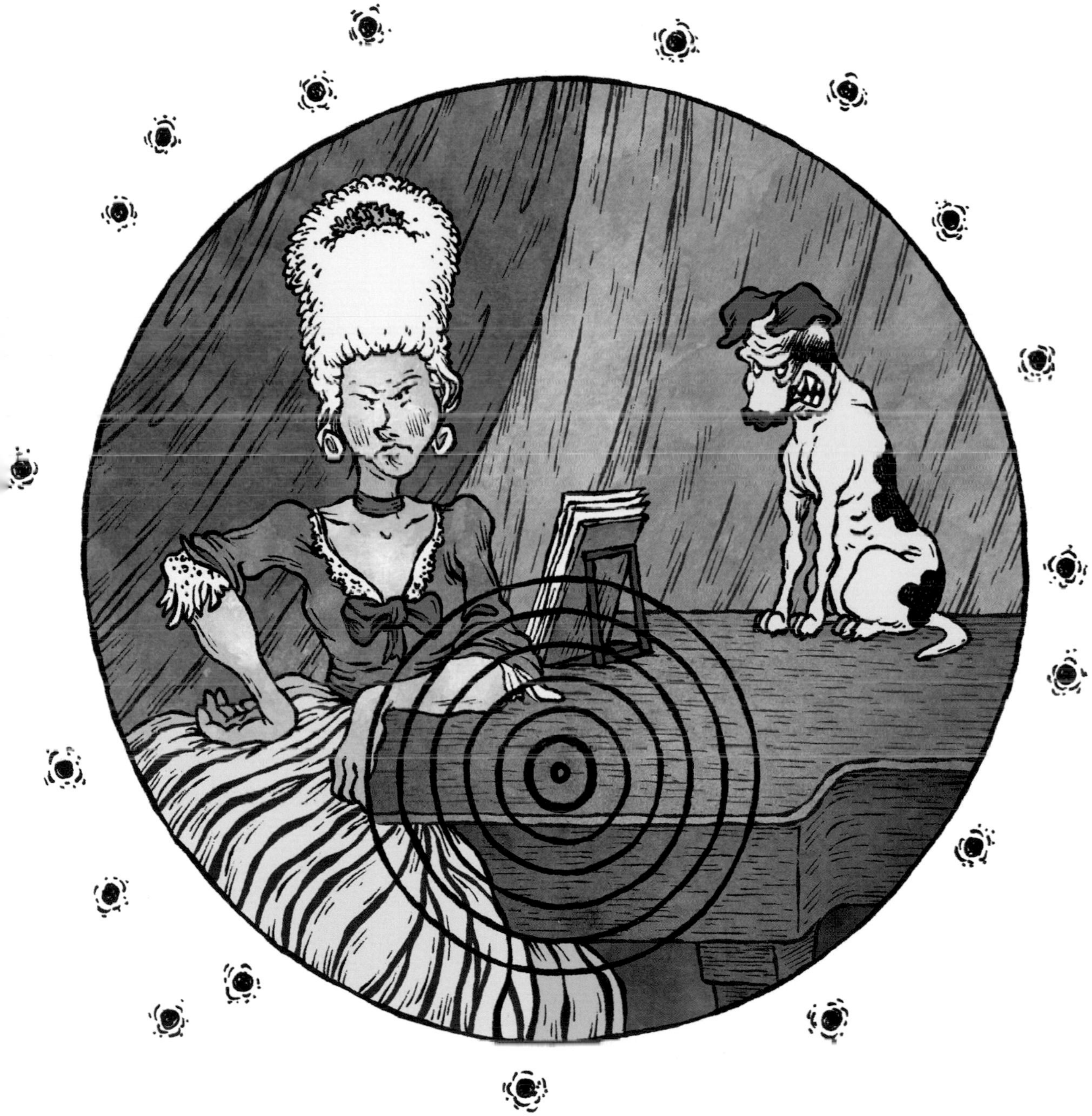

The Gift

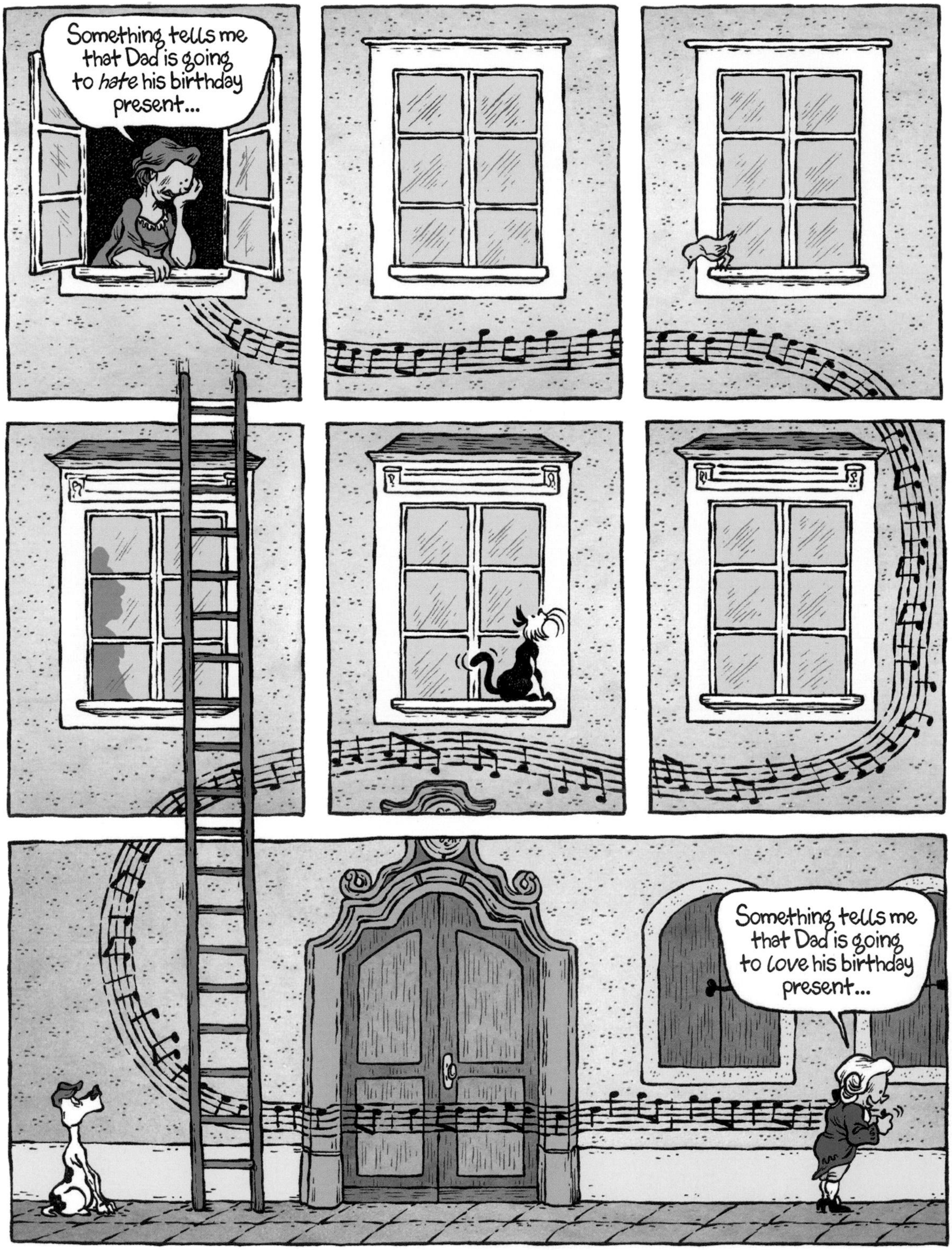

Something tells me that Dad is going to *hate* his birthday present...
Something tells me that Dad is going to *love* his birthday present...

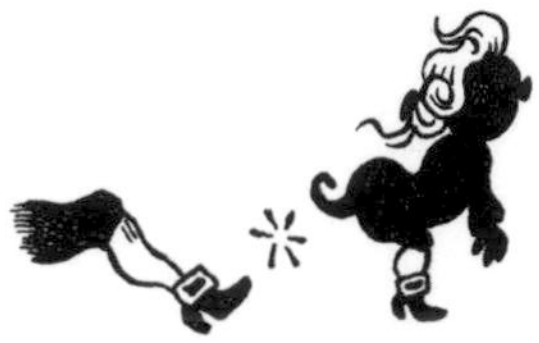

Player No More

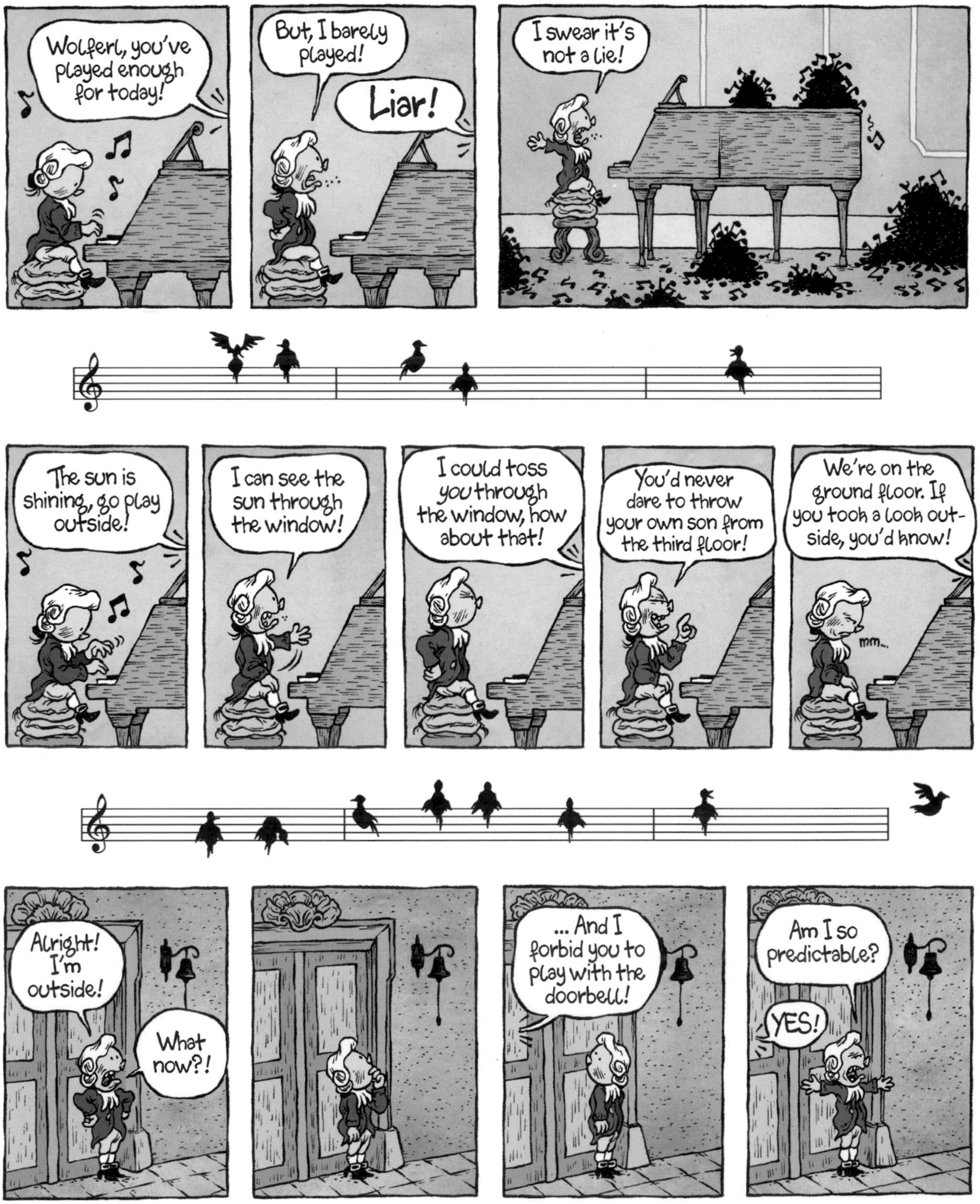
Wolferl, you've played enough for today!
But, I barely played!
Liar!
I swear it's not a lie!
The sun is shining, go play outside!
I can see the sun through the window!
I could toss you through the window, how about that!
You'd never dare to throw your own son from the third floor!
We're on the ground floor. If you took a look out-side, you'd know!
mm...
Alright! I'm outside!
What now?!
... And I forbid you to play with the doorbell!
Am I so predictable?
YES!

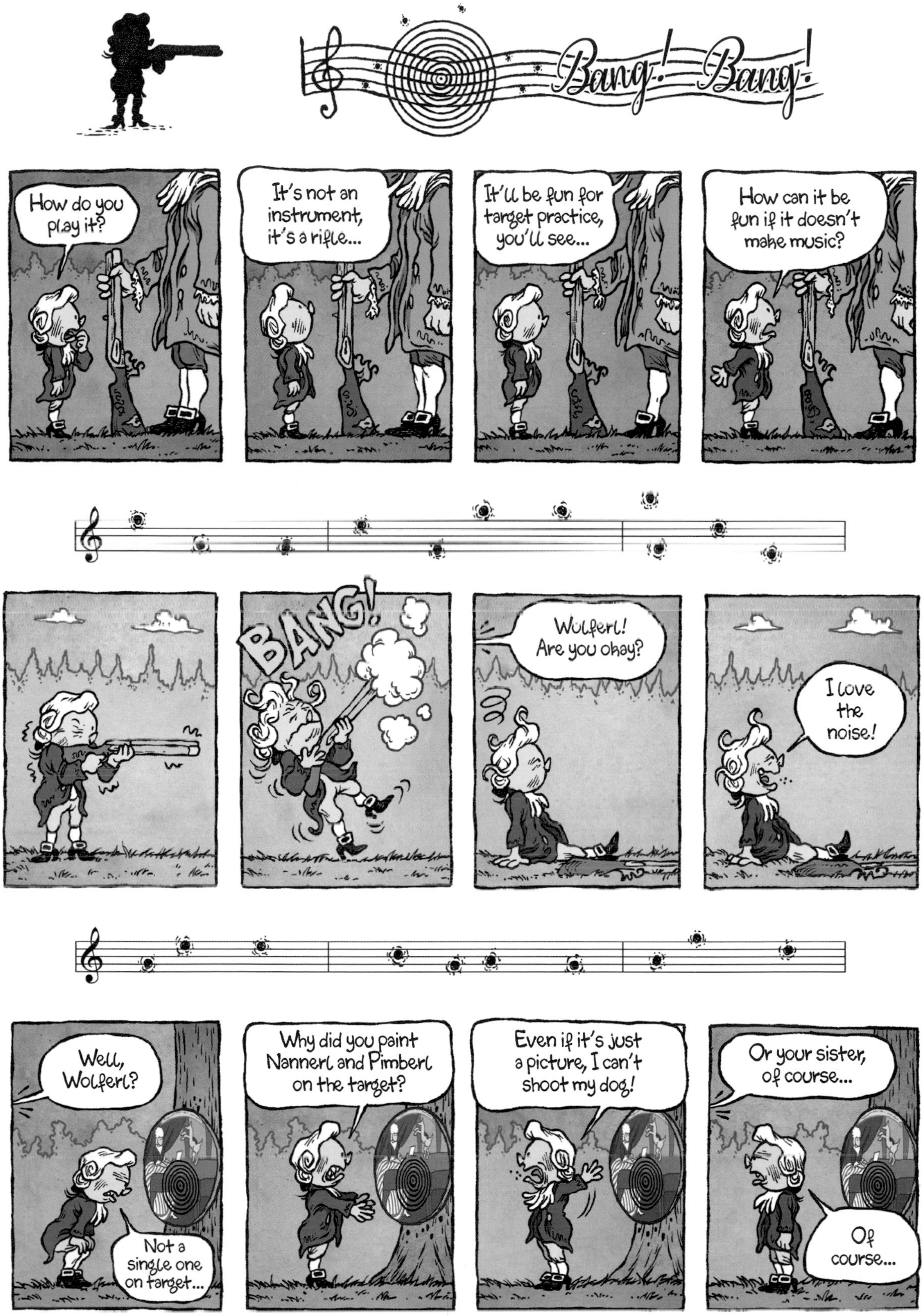
Bang! Bang!
How do you play it?
It's not an instrument, it's a rifle...
It'll be fun for target practice, you'll see...
How can it be fun if it doesn't make music?
BANG!
Wolferl! Are you okay?
I love the noise!
Well, Wolferl?
Not a single one on target...
Why did you paint Nannerl and Pimberl on the target?
Even if it's just a picture, I can't shoot my dog!
Or your sister, of course...
Of course...

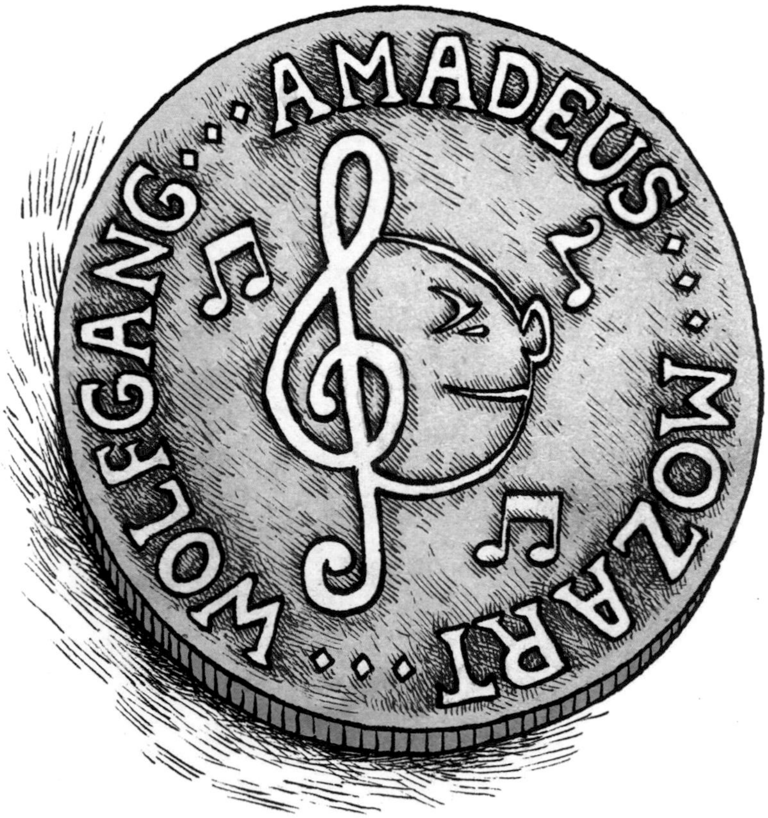
WOLFGANG AMADEUS MOZART

Young Mozart's Playbook

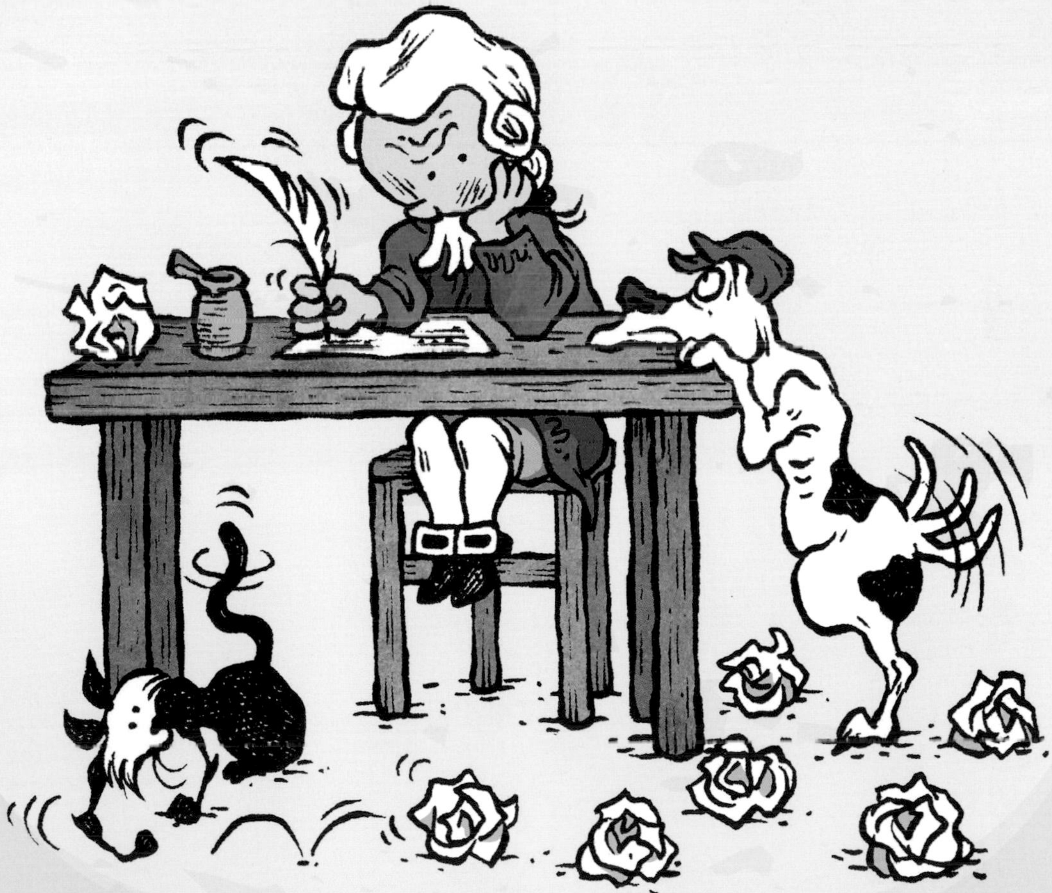

MusiQuiz

How familiar are you with music vocabulary? Here's a little test! Pair the right word with its definition and you'll see how well-versed you are...

1 Allegro

2 Score

3 Soprano

4 Melody

5 Bass

6 Symphony

7 Chord

8 Cantata

9 Acoustics

10 Harmony

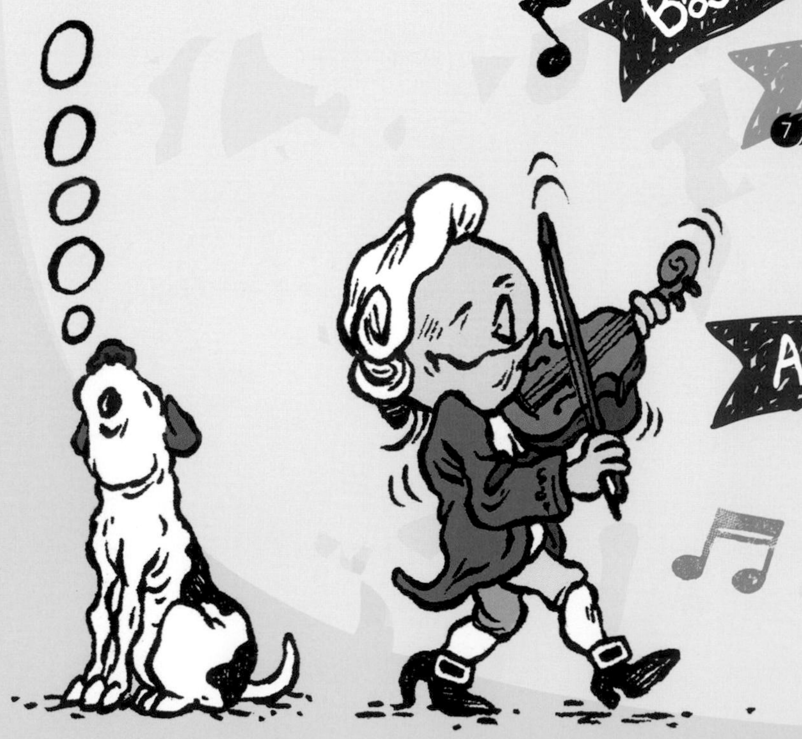

NSWERS: 1-A, 2-I, 3-H, 4-E, 5-C, 6-J, 7-F, 8-D, 9-B, 10-G

A Fast paced. A piece of music that is meant to be played quickly.

B Qualities of a room or building that determine how sound is transmitted in it.

C The lowest male voice in a chorus. Also, a very low sounding instrument.

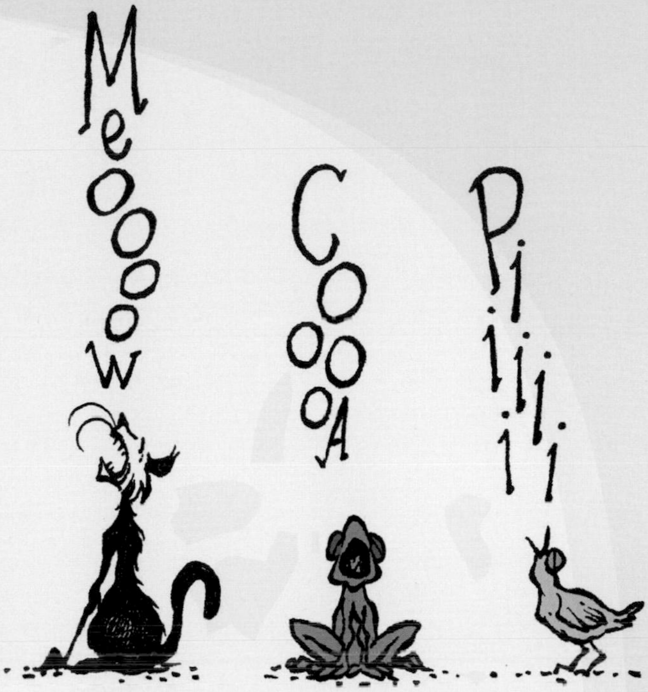
Meooooow
CooooA
Piiiii

D A piece of music written to be performed by both vocalists and instrumental musicians.

H The highest female voice in a chorus. Also, the highest pitched instrument.

E A sequence of notes and rhythms.

I A music manuscript which includes the parts for each instrument.

J An orchestra, or a composition for a large orchestra.

F Three or more notes played at the same time.

G The sounding of two or more notes at the same time.

SCOREBOX

10 GOOD ANSWERS! You're musical genius level! Mozart would be proud of you.

6-9 GOOD ANSWERS! You're a standard! A little extra knowledge and you'll be a reference!

1-5 GOOD ANSWERS! You're a Basic Chord in the field. Don't panic. The best of us started there!

Word Search

Cross all the names below (horizontal, vertical and even backwards!) and get to know Mozart's most famous music. Then, find the mystery word in the grid...

A	A	P	A	N	T	O	M	I	M	E	O	I	F
D	F	N	G	I	M	N	U	O	R	E	O	O	U
G	A	V	O	T	T	E	M	I	A	O	G	O	G
R	E	T	M	L	I	A	R	E	S	T	T	P	U
T	T	H	E	M	A	G	I	C	F	L	U	T	E
O	R	G	M	M	I	T	R	I	D	A	T	E	S
Y	R	O	T	C	I	V	S	G	R	U	B	O	C
O	R	N	D	S	O	G	V	E	F	A	O	E	G
U	O	A	I	D	O	M	E	N	E	O	P	G	L
O	A	N	L	N	T	I	E	I	N	U	U	G	F
D	T	N	N	C	T	E	I	A	V	N	N	A	N
C	T	E	B	A	N	N	E	R	L	E	M	P	I
T	G	R	D	O	N	G	I	O	V	A	N	N	I
C	N	L	O	S	I	F	A	N	T	U	T	T	E

DON GIOVANNI
Composed in 1787 and based on a legendary Italian character.

MITRIDATE
Composed in 1770 while Mozart was touring Italy.

THE MAGIC FLUTE
One of Mozart's most famous operas, and the last he wrote.

IDOMENEO
An opera from 1781, commissioned for a court carnaval.

NANNERL
"Nannerl's Music Book" is a set of compositions written by Mozart's dad for his daughter from 1759 to 1764. Mozart himself contributed to and played it.

SERAIL
In German, *Die Entführung aus dem Serail (Abduction at the Seraglio)*, another very famous 3 acts opera from 1781.

PANTOMIME
"Pantomime" is a piece written in 1767 as part of *The Little Nothings* ballet.

COSI FAN TUTTE
An opera Mozart debuted in January 1790.

GAVOTTE
A French dance from the 18th century. Mozart wrote a few of those.

COBURG'S VICTORY
A short famous tune from 1789, also known as "Contredanse for orchestra in C major- K.587."

The Mystery Word

What you have to find can be defined as a composition in which a short melody or phrase is introduced by one part then successively taken up by other parts. It's a...

F ... ...

82

The Sound of Music

Mozart has lost his violin! Help him find it by following the sound of music. Pick the right path to get to our musician's beloved instrument. And watch out! Don't hit any wrong notes along the way!

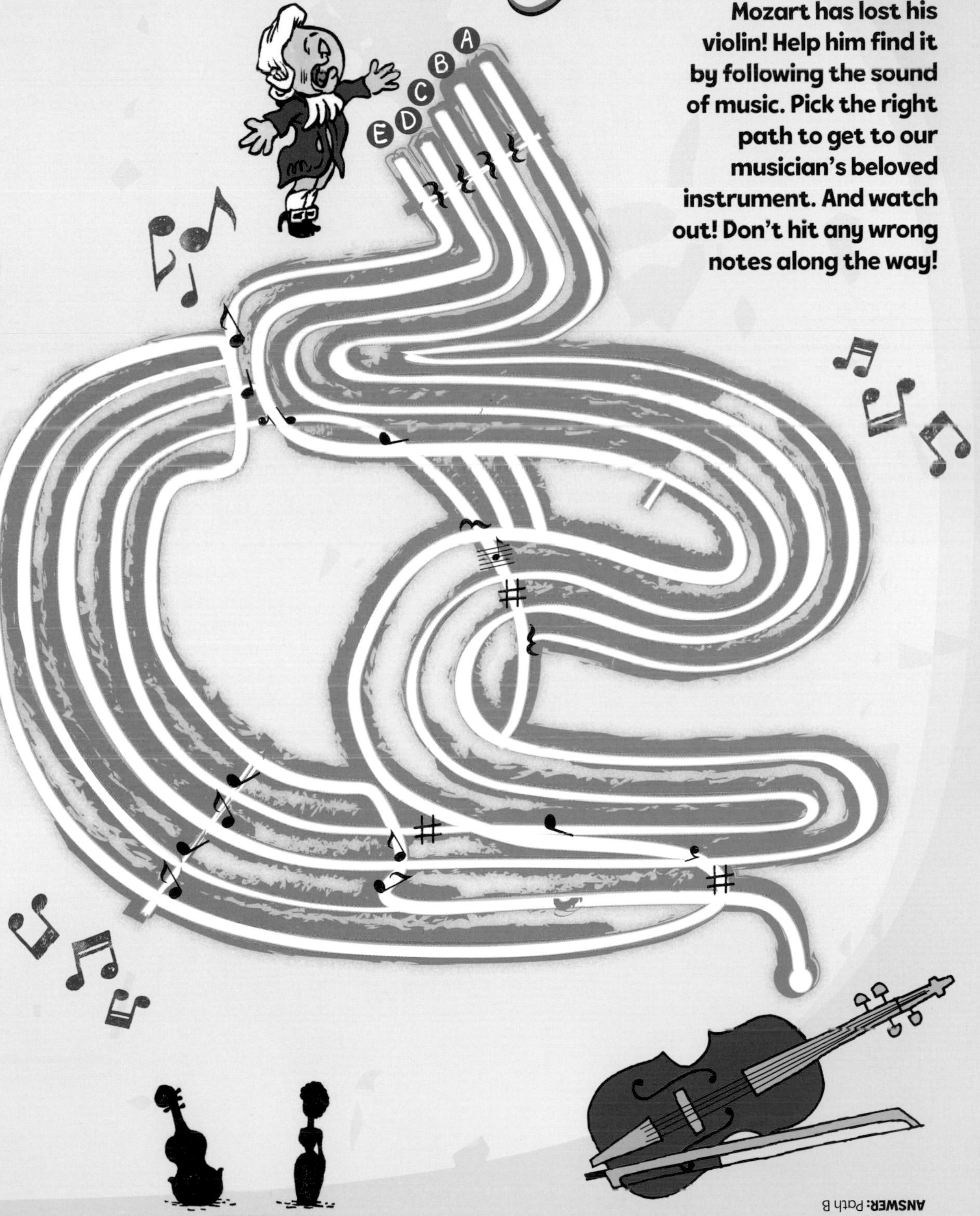
E
D
C
B
A

ANSWER: Path B

Mozart Wiki

How familiar are you with Mozart? Here's an opportunity to learn more about the musical wunderkind...

January
27

We know him as **Wolfgang Amadeus Mozart** but his full name is Johannes Chrysostomus Wolfgangus Theophilus Mozart (and you thought *your* first name was long?). He was born on January 27th, 1756.

AUSTRIA
Vienna
Linz
Salzburg
Innsbruck
Graz
Eisenstadt
Klagenfurt
Bregenz
Gmund
Poysdorf
Scharding
Wiener Neustadt
Kitzbühel
Bischofshofen
Leoben
Kapfenberg
Knittelfeld
Villach
Deutschlandsberg
Bludenz
Landeck
Lienz
Fürstenfeld

He was born in **Salzburg**, Austria. This country is a rather small one in Europe, located between Germany, Switzerland and Italy.

Mozart was a child prodigy. He started composing music at the **age of five**. He finished his first symphony when he was only eight years old and wrote his first opera at fourteen years old.

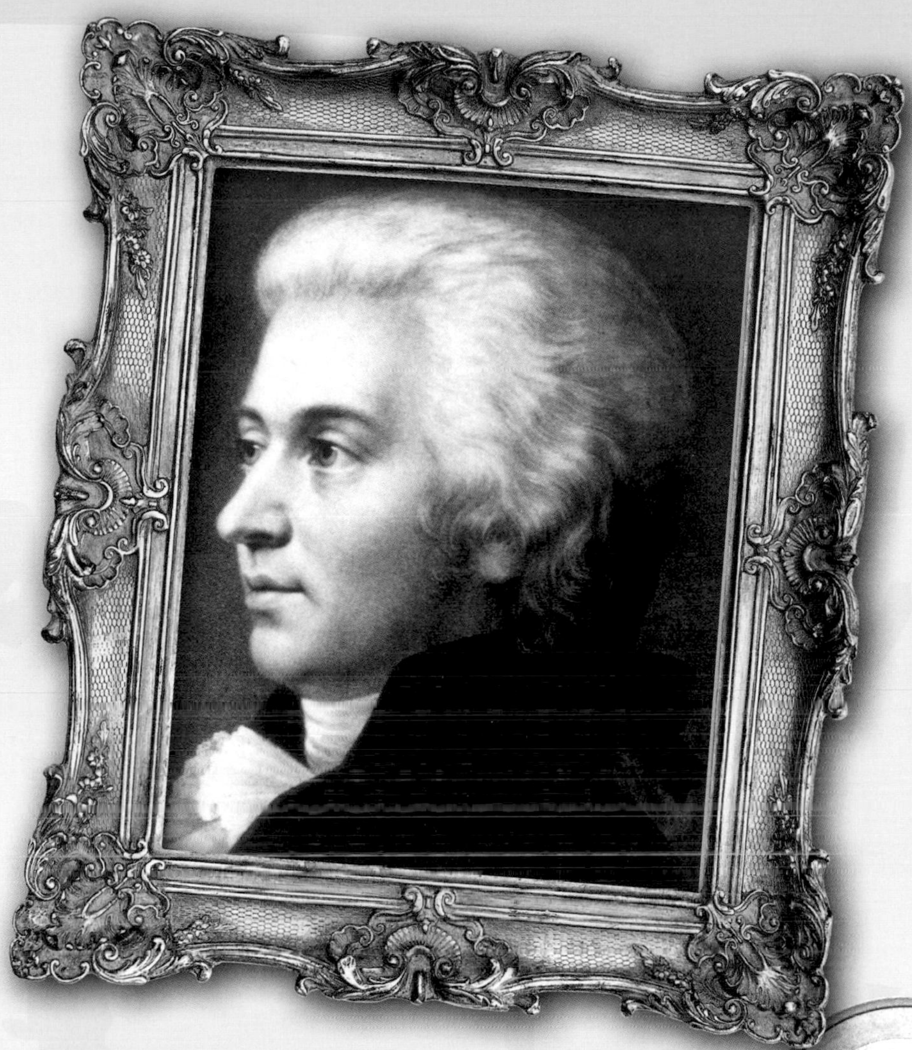

He composed over **600 musical works** in his lifetime. He played both violin and piano. He could play the piano backwards and blindfolded.

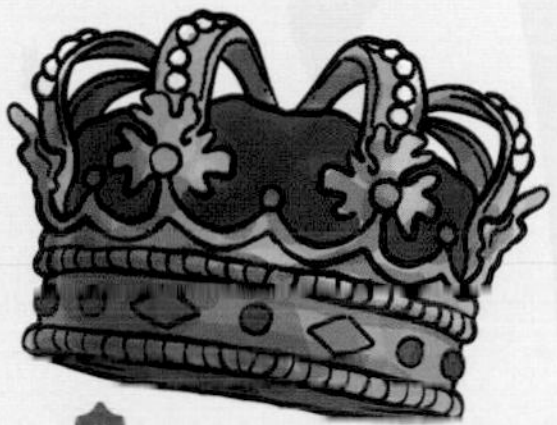

By the time he was six years old, he had already performed for **royalty**.

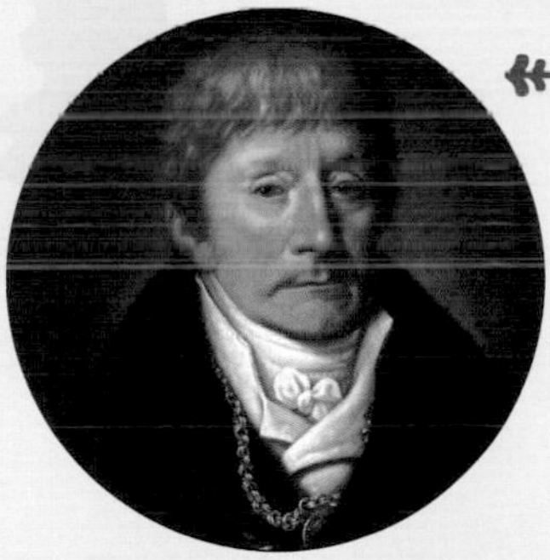

Painting by Joseph Willibrord Mähler

Antonio Salieri was Mozart's lifelong rival, but respected him nonetheless. He was one of the few to attend Mozart's funeral and even gave music lessons to his son.

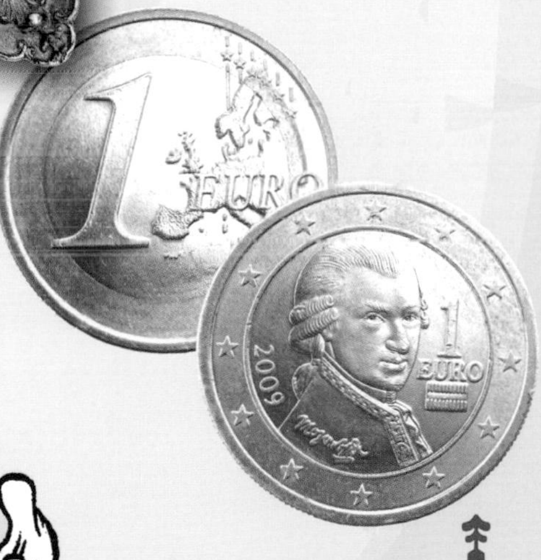
1
EURO
2009
1 EURO

The Austrian €1 coin has Mozart on it!

Divertimento for two horns and string quartet is thought to have been written as an intentionally funny, over-repetitive piece. It is often referred to as **A Musical Joke**. Yes, Mozart seemed to have a great sense of humor!

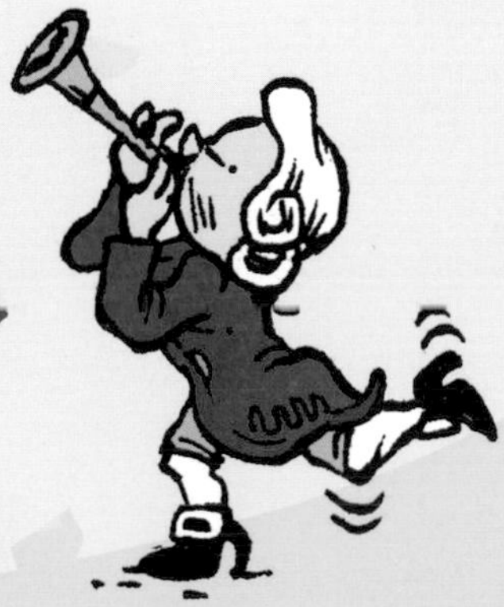

The Right Shadow

Sometimes, it seems as though Mozart's shadow has a life of its own! Shaking, bouncing and dancing to the sound of music... Can you find the matching shadows from the illustrations below?

ANSWER: A and E are the same.

What's in a Note?

A note is a **musical sound** or **written symbol**.
There are different kinds of notes:

WHOLE NOTE
A note with four beats

HALF NOTE
A note with two beats

QUARTER NOTE
A note with one beat

How can we combine them?

A) _____ + _____ = (half note)

B) ___ + ___ + ___ + ___ = (whole note)

C) ___ + ___ + ___ = (whole note)

D) _____ - _____ = (half note)

Think about how many beats there are in each note to find the answers!

ANSWERS: A) Quarter Note + Quarter Note= Half Note B) Quarter Note + Quarter Note + Quarter Note + Quarter Note= Whole Note C) Quarter Note + Quarter Note + Half Note= Whole Note D) Whole Note - Half Note= Half Note.

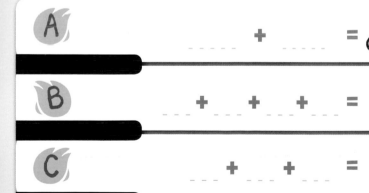

To make learning fun is the goal of every parent and educator. With a combination of humor and history, *Young Mozart* makes a great addition to your home, library, and classroom.

For additional educational materials like Teacher's Guides and more visit:
https://bit.ly/2UWtBvX